Dedicated to all who served. Thank you for the safety we enjoy because of your willingness to keep us safe.

If you would like to know more about the author and the series you can find me at lawrence'sletters@wordress.com

Sting of the Scorpion

Prologue

Istanbul, present day

The train was running on time which was and yet wasn't unusual. It was for this part of the globe. Very little in the Middle East runs to a timetable, yet it wasn't unusual really as the Turkish rail system being modelled on the ultra-efficient German rail networks that pride themselves in running an efficient system, guaranteeing your arrival time to within five minutes no matter how long the journey, and in Turkey there are quite a few journeys that take a hefty chunk out of a day, even with trains fast enough to rival most of Europe's networks.

Steve had boarded the train in Ankara at 8 am and had taken a 'continental breakfast' with croissants and a delicious coffee on the train. The traditional Middle Eastern breakfast of Goat feta, olives, and bread with a dipping sauce of Tahina had been on offer, but the coffee had smelled too good to pass up, so he'd chosen that one.

Six hours later the train was pulling into the station and he was hungry again, but satisfying that hunger would have to wait until he found the place he was meeting his contact.

The station was just like any train station worldwide, busy people running everywhere. No one really taking in what was all around them, except the tourists who were taking pictures of everything, and from the look of them Steve guessed that they were Asians, probably Japanese or Koreans who took pictures of everything that moved, he often wondered just what it was they saw that garnered enough interest that they wanted a permanent record of it, but then again maybe everything was so different that a picture was needed to show the folks back home!

Two years working in the British Embassy in Ankara had cured him of that, and then some! Now he saw, yet didn't see the things around him. He saw the history of the place and enjoyed it, yet the whole place was just a part of the job now and most of the time it was just "there" the amazing Byzantine architecture alongside modern functional concrete buildings that just looked as if they'd always fitted together.

The cab rank was slightly to the right as you left the main building, the distinctive yellow of the cabs were not sure if they were meant to copy the New York cabs (Turks loved to copy things like that and try to make the tourist feel at home so they'll feel safer spending more money!) a half dozen of them were waiting on the rank.

Walking up to the first one he opened the door and climbed in, "Merhaba" he greeted the driver in Turkish, "Topkapi please" the driver muttered a greeting back then leaned over and pressed a few buttons to start his meter then putting the car into gear set off.

The ride would work out expensive, but he wasn't paying so he wasn't worried. One of the great things working for the government was the travel was almost always of Whitehall's tab and that was just fine with him, mind you this trip was all business at least until tonight when he would indulge himself a little at one of the many bars that cater for the tourist that he'd keep to himself so it would be all 'cash up front.

It made him think of the famous saying from Kipling. 'East is east, West is west and ne'er the twain shall meet until earth and sky and sea shall meet beneath Gods judgement seat'. "He never saw Istanbul," he thought to himself with a smile.

The trip would take about fifteen minutes, normally it would be time to run through things but today it was simple, he'd gotten a call last night from a contact telling him to meet in Istanbul at the 'usual place' no time had been given but they had a system for working that out, the last meeting had been at noon so their next meeting would be at three pm the following day, a simple system really. Always between the hours of six am and nine pm and always three hours after the time of the previous one, so if the last one was at noon then the next was at three and the one after would be at six pm until you got to nine pm when the next would be at six in the morning!

Neither Steve or the cabbie saw the small red car following them, then again if they had they wouldn't have worried at the middle-aged female driver in the car, but she was interested in them.

"Yellow Taxi number 2541" she spoke into the phone she was holding, she hung up and put the car into gear

Cheltenham, England

Someone is always listening, no matter where the call is made and at what time you make it someone is listening. Big Brother really exists and he was listening in to that call, not that the call was interesting but it was who took the call that the computers in GCHQ Cheltenham were interested in.

The computers logged the call and sent an email to an analyst to listen in to the recording to make a decision as to whether there needed to be 'follow up' but for now nothing else was done.

Istanbul

The red car didn't follow the Taxicab, there wasn't any need and they knew the pattern. Instead, she made her own way to Topkapi and parked just a few blocks from a coffee shop that had a mix of tourists and locals.

Istanbul is the place where East and West not only meet but so do the ancient and modern, instead of it being an assault on the senses that occurs in other places somehow Istanbul managed to blend them all into a unique flavour that can be and is enjoyed by all. The latest fashion in the most modern of department stores sitting right next to the ancient bazaars selling the traditional and ancient things which Turkey is famous for, and all sitting right next to some of the greatest monuments of the Eastern and Western world!

The Topkapi Palace, just across the Bosphorus from the Saint Sophia Museum and one of the most magnificent scenes that anyone can see, the place where the tourist attractions famous all over the globe meet with the humble coffee shops that are almost as famous as the icons that bring people from the far corners.

Steve loved the view from the coffee shop, he could sit in the back of the shop and take in some of the most famous places in the world, he could literally watch the world go by from where he was, but he wasn't here for that he was here to meet a contact, a mid-level 'soldier' in one of Turkey's drug gangs, one who said he could tell them the new routes that the drug barons are taking in getting the drugs to Europe and that was what today's meet was about.

The small red car had morphed into a green one, at first glance no one would have known that they were the same vehicle, but first glances were all that people were going to get, the middle-aged woman parked the car about fifty meters from the coffee shop, got out and began walking away, as soon as she got to the end of the street she reached into her bag, took out a mobile phone and pressed a number.

The street erupted into a ball of flame as the car leapt into the air and came crashing down a good fifteen meters nearer to the coffee shop. The bomb had been in three places all designed to detonate at the same time, both front doors packed with explosives turned into small fragments of shrapnel and shredded everything and everyone for twenty meters on both sides of the street, the Engine, where the bulk of the C4 had been separated from the gearbox and flew fifty meters down the street smashing into a top of the range Mercedes killing its occupants, a junior minister, his bodyguard and his driver instantly.

The front of the shop disappeared in a ball of flame, the German tourists were still sat at their tables, but one was killed instantly as the flying shrapnel decapitated him, his girlfriend sat there stunned for a few seconds then started screaming at her headless boyfriend not realising her arm had been completely severed and she had only a few more seconds to live herself before she 'bled out'. The waiter who'd just served Steve was killed instantly by the fireball his body slumped and ablaze at the front of the shop.

The natural reaction is to run, flee in a panic and run right into whatever mayhem might be happening outside, some would stay and in a daze begin to look for those they could help, if there were any.

Training kicked in, the stuff that he'd learned for his job and was told to make it second nature, everything in his being wanted to stop and help the wounded, but a voice was telling him "You're the target here, and you need to get out fast, they're coming back for you!"

He slowly rose to his feet, half acting as if he was in shock and half in a daze, he began feeling his way around, dust and flames were everywhere, at the back of the shop the oven was burning out of control and some furniture was beginning to catch fire, he had seconds to make it to the back door before that exit was blocked, he began to move quickly, but not quick enough.

The other men began to move, in the pandemonium he'd forgotten about them, only now did he see the danger as one wrapped his arms around his neck in a vice-like headlock "Mr Chambers" one of the others spoke in heavily accented English, a third took out a syringe and gently inserted it into his neck, quickly succumbing to whatever was in it the last thing he remembered hearing was the man saying "You have so much to tell us!"

Chapter one.

Scorpion team.

"Where are you?" the phone wasn't even at his ear when he heard those words, and the voice was unmistakable.

"Boss" he replied, "Nice to hear from you again, how long's it been? Two hours?" Joey knew this wasn't good!

"Cut the chit chat, Joey, by my reckoning you're at the pub now, just parked the car at home and straight round for a few at the Park Lane tavern if I'm right?" Joey instinctively looked around the room as it was as if Jacko was watching him, in a sense he was but not from the room, he was watching a computer screen that showed Joey's GPS coordinates from the phone he was using.

"You got that Boss, just arrived and just sinking my first one why?"

"Sorry mate, you'll have to cut it short" Jacko being apologetic meant something was seriously wrong, what the hell could it be? "We're wanted and pronto in London"

"Shit" Joey started to reply "I've only just gone on leave, a leave that's about three months overdue remember boss"

"My heart bleeds for you! Now get your arse into gear, there's a 'cab' in the way for you, be at St George's Park on Windmill Street in fifteen" the phone went dead.

"Shit" was all he could think, he skulled the pint he'd just ordered, took out a couple of pound coins slapped them on the bar and started to run out the door, "Sorry Geoff, gotta run" and he was gone at full sprint.

Geoff, the barman and owner scooped the money into the till thinking "Where the hell's he off to now?" not that they'd get the chance to ask!

Joey rounded the corner just as the 'cab' was coming in, an Augusta eight-seater that looked just like any other corporate helicopter, anyone seeing it would think some exec getting a lift back to the office, except this was a working-class neighbourhood and rich corporate execs don't show up sprinting for all they're worth at dusk to climb into strange aircraft. The Augusta may be an eight-seater but he noticed only three seats were filled, a fourth was empty and the rest had equipment bags in them

"Glad you could fit us in" Jacko was the first to speak as he buckled himself in. He handed Joey a headset, not that there'd be much talking on the flight, more to protect the ears from the noise of the engines.

"Thanks for the invite boss, next time can you give me a bit of warning!" Joey shot back, one thing he loved about this outfit was the Regiment didn't stand on ceremony; if you got crap from them you simply gave it back, no matter the rank "What's up anyway?"

"No idea really" it was one of the others, Mac a large red headed Scotsman with the temper to match spoke up "As usual"

"True enough" Jacko interjected, "We've just been told to get the hell down to London and we'll be told what it's all about there, your kit's in the bags" he pointed to the two bags by Joey's seat, he didn't mean clothes. Turning to the aircrew he flicked open their channel "You know where we're going boys, we're in your hands" he said with a slight smile.

"No worries Jacko" the pilot replied "We've got you covered, all we can say is it's by Vauxhall Bridge" They didn't need to say more, there's only one government building fits that description Vauxhall house the HQ for MI6.

Cheshire to London is about a hundred and sixty miles, five hours by road but just under an hour by air if you take a direct route, they were flying under five thousand feet and that's Military airspace, no need for a flight plan and no need to muck around.

Forty-five minutes later the first words after the greetings were spoken, "Twenty miles out" The pilot turned to the aircrewman, "Time to light us up" darkness had closed in but he didn't mean navigation lights. The crewman leaned forward and flicked a switch on his console "I.F.F. on" He spoke quietly to all, "they'll see us in a minute" he pulled a small screen down from the overhead console, it came to life as he pulled away, a small green light came on at the side of the screen. "They have us, we're good to go!"

I.F.F. stands for "Identify Friend or Foe and is a similar system to what all fighter planes use to 'talk' to friendly radar, a more downmarket version is used for civilian air traffic, this was a bit more advanced.

Most Londoners think that the 'Ring of steel' air defences were put around London for the London Olympics, they weren't, they've always been there, the difference is they only guard certain places in London, Parliament doesn't get it, but Downing Street and Vauxhall Bridge both get protection along with a few other places, all what happened during the Olympics was it was expanded and some of the sites weren't taken down as promised, it was the IFF that had just locked on, identified them as friends and let them through, no one contemplated what might happen if they didn't get identified as there would be no warning, just a downed helicopter and six dead soldiers.

Joey looked out the side window, he could see a Police helicopter in the distance moving up and down, he figured the Police chopper was about ten miles away (at night at this height the navigation lights can be seen that far away) and by the way it was flying it was checking the traffic on the M1 motorway heading north, probably not even aware they were in the air. The Police chopper also had the I.F.F. fitted but clear orders not to stray from their route. besides Thames House kept an eye on even the 'allowed traffic' and any violation would not be good for the one who breaks the rule!

As soon as the skids touched the pilot began shutdown procedure, it took about fifteen seconds to stop the blades turning, they were getting out when they saw a guy running towards them with wheels under his arms, as they entered the building they saw him clamping the wheels to the skids, a quick levering using a pole he brought with him and they were mobile wheeling the machine, he and the two aircrew were manhandling the aircraft into the small hanger on the roof that looked just like a penthouse within three minutes there was no trace there'd ever been a helipad on the roof.

The four of them walked through the building in silence. They knew where they were going, the operations centre or 'Ops' as they sometimes called it (or Oops when there'd been a screw-up, more often than not it was the Oops centre when the proverbial hit the fan!

"This way please gents" a clear female voice spoke out in the stillness, moments later a head appeared out of a doorway, the head belonged to a very attractive redhead, it disappeared as quickly as it had appeared.

The door was to 'Briefing room 2' or at least that's what it said on the door, but what lay before them was unlike any briefing room in the Army! A large LED screen made up the far wall; it was showing news feed from the situation in Turkey, except it wasn't the news playing. The screen went blank as they entered.

In front of the screen was a long dark table, it looked like oak, but that could be just a veneer, around the table were seven chairs, all leather and the three at the head had occupants, the redhead was on the third chair.

"Take a seat boys" the man at the head of the table, an older man in a grey suit, the kind of one you wouldn't notice on a busy day spoke quietly, "Welcome to our little place"

The four of them took seats without saying a word, no need really, they all knew where they were and it was about to become obvious as to why besides you get to know who the director of MI6 is even if you never meet him in person. "Glad you invited us Sir Michael" Jacko spoke for the team.

"Captain Jackson" Sir Michael replied, "How much do you and your men know about the situation in Turkey?"

"Are we speaking about the Bombs in Istanbul sir?" he asked, "If that's the case only what the news media has told the public". There was a jug of water on the table in front of them, Joey, as the junior in the squad leaned over and taking the four glasses lined them up and began to pour four glasses of cold water, starting with Jacko they each reached out taking a glass. "I take it there's more to the story?"

"Very much so" The redhead took over, "with your permission Sir Michael?" it was clear she was taking over the briefing.

"Do carry on Sandy" Sir Michael handed the rest over to Sandy, short for Sandra, a career intelligence officer that the team had dealt with previously, very good at her job and as the red hair indicated one not to be tangled with, she was fairly new to the position and by all accounts had only been with '6' a couple of years.

Sandra Little, a graduate of Oxford "Where all the best operatives come from" she'd pointed out to the team, that was until Joey had pointed out that Philby, Burgess and McLean the three most notorious traitors in British history had also come from there!

"Actually they went to Cambridge" she shot back smiling.

At five feet eight inches Joey figured Sandy was just three or four inches shorter than he was, he guessed her height from the fact he had to look down slightly when talking to her. Hourglass figure, yet she was trying to hide it under a jumper and slacks that were slightly too big and consequently baggy on her, she wasn't wearing makeup, but the red hair set against the pale white skin that accentuated the fine features of her bone structure, Joey was totally smitten, but at the same time was telling himself "You haven't got a prayer!"

"The Bombs were a cover for something else" Sandy began.

"Forty-five dead, sixty injured and that's only a cover?" Mac spoke up. "Remind me not to piss these folks off too often" in most military units Mac would be silenced smartly, not with the Regiment, as in the SAS everyone speaks their mind and 'Officers' better get used to it. Both Sir Michael and Sandy had worked with them before and they knew what to expect, the man in uniform was 'the boss' Lieutenant Colonel Peter Simpson.

"Shows how important the target was to them" it was colonel Simpson spoke up. "Listen up boys." The LED screen came to life with a giant picture of a man. "Meet Steve Chambers, sorry Sandy but I know Steve, hope you don't mind me doing the intros" he continued on, "Until last year he was our liaison with '6' and a bloody good man for a spook" Sandy couldn't help a small smile as that was high praise coming from him.

"We knew Chambers" Jacko replied, "If he's in trouble you've come to the right place, we were all mates with him"

"Bit more than just 'in trouble' I'm afraid" Sandy took back over, "Chambers had a meet at that Coffee shop at that time, and he was there when the bombs went off"

"Bad luck" Jacko spoke up, "But if he's killed or injured why the need for?"

"He's not dead" Sandy headed him off, "Least not yet as far as we know, and he's not there anymore!"

"Isis planted the Bombs right?" Joey spoke for the first time in the meeting, "Was he working on something linked to them?"

"That's what Turkey's told the world" Sandy replied, "But it's not the whole picture!"
She pressed a button on the remote she'd just picked up, a new picture came up. "Remember him?"

"Al Jabbari" the four almost spoke in unison, "one of the most feared Bomb makers of the Iraqi uprising, and someone thought dead! "Jeez boss, what next?" Joey carried on for all of them. "You going to tell us Saddam's still alive? Or is it Osama?"

"Neither," Sandy spoke up, she'd been sitting but at this point, she stood and walked round to the front of the table. That's when Joey noticed she was wearing flat shoes, he couldn't help himself thinking about her, but telling himself she was 'way out of his league'. Sandy went on, "But it seems that the Yanks may have missed with an airstrike or two" she flicked another slide up, "the signature is the same, so he may also have changed paymasters!" she pointed to the screen, it was a series of names, dates and places with what looked like figures of some kind of material besides them; "This is a rundown of interceptions of quantities of heroin in the last year, take a look at the amounts"

"Quite a few kilos" they were all impressed, but Jacko was the one vocalised it.

"That's not kilos" Sandy replied, that's how many truckloads were seized, or rather consignments over ten kilograms!"

"Pretty impressive" Smithy, a quiet northerner with a lanky frame and a ready smile finally spoke up, "but what's it got to do with us today?"

"Chambers was the one gathering the intelligence." Sandy came back with a quick reply, she switched the machine off and leaned against it eyeing each of them in turn, she paused for effect, and it was electric. "He's got contacts feeding him the information as to when and where the drugs were coming in" she paused again. "Naturally they got suspicious as to where he got his info from"

"So they took him out, or tried to?"

"No!" Sir Michael spoke sharply, "We think they kidnapped him for information, or they had him taken"

It took a moment before the boys took it in, "So he's alive, and you think they'll squeeze him for the information?" Jacko spoke up, "Let's cut to the chase here Sir Mike, this is a Rescue or Destroy then isn't it?"

'Rescue or Destroy' often known as 'RoD' missions, where an operative with vital intelligence is captured by the other side, the intelligence they've got often so vital it could literally tip the balance of power and makes it critical that they not fall into enemy hands, if they do then the order is given to either get them back or eliminate them! It's a last resort and everyone hates them, "pity the poor sod who has to carry 'em out" Jacko knew his team would perform miracles rather than carry one out.

They'd heard of the order before, but only in the distant past when war was raging, now in peacetime they were being told to prep for an 'RoD' mission.

Another screen came up with a list of names, most of which looked European, but there were a few Middle Eastern and Slavic among them.

"Those names you see there," Sir Michael's voice was so quiet you'd think he knew the drug barons were listening in, "They're the names of the people we've arrested, before we arrested them, or at least before we let it be known they were in custody, we looked into their Bank accounts"

"And?"

"We moved some of the money and took a look at both whom it was sent to afterwards and where it came from originally" Sir Michael went on, "You understand I'm telling you way more than I need to don't you?"

"I think you understand Sir Michael" the Colonel spoke up for his men, "You give an order for us to kill one of our own and we damn well want to know why?" he wasn't angry, but there was a firmness in his voice"

"Three hundred million pounds and counting" Sir Michael explained, "And that's as far as we know at the moment!" He stopped mid-sentence to see what they were thinking, they were computing how many nights on the town that lot would pay for, quite a few years. "Not dollars! Not to mention all the linked accounts we found out about!" he finally finished the sentence when he saw the figures sink in.

"Not a lot then?" Joey was trying to make light of the situation, the others didn't even think about the situation "Stealing from the drug barons, no wonder!"

Most military units work on the junior ranks doing what the senior ranks say no matter how dumb it might be, the SAS is different, with the 'Regiment' everyone has a say and everyone can say exactly what they think, Sir Michael knew it, and MI6 had too many dealings with the Regiment not to respect it no matter how much it ran against the grain, they got things done, and that's what mattered.

But an R.O.D was hard to swallow especially for one of your own, and Steve Chambers was one of theirs, he was a mate, they didn't say it but the expressions said it all "Hell will freeze over first!"

"Where is he now?" Jacko was getting back to business, "Any ideas?"

"Actually yes" Sandy broke in, "Chambers has a body tracker installed, and it's still active so we assume he's still attached to it meaning his head is still on his shoulders"

"R.F.I.D. tracker?" Jacko asked curiously.

"Inserted under the shoulder blades" Sandy replied. "Surgically installed and powered by the body's own electrical grid, stop the electrical power and the system shuts off" she carried on. "That happens and we know he's dead!"

"Where is he then?" they were only interested in the job at hand.

"It's not where he is that's the worry Sandy spoke as she pressed a button on the desk, a screen descended from the ceiling, "This is secret enough that we don't store the information together, we're more worried about where he's going, take a look"

The screen came to life with a video, a bleak and forbidding landscape with a jagged mountain range. The buildings looked like a monastery with three sides protected by sheer cliff faces, the fourth had an access path, it would be too ambitious to call it a road, but there was some form of access that looked like a donkey track. "Welcome to the assassins' fortress" Sandy spoke quietly.

"Getting poetic Sandy?" Jacko almost smiled as he leaned forward to get a closer look, "The land looks like Iran?"

"You're right in one way" she replied. "But not with the poetry" she stood up and pointed to the building on the hill with a laser pointer, "This actually is the assassins fortress at Alamut in North West Iran"

"Thought that was just in the movies" Joey was almost smirking, "You know, Bruce Willis and all that stuff?" he leaned forward tapping the top of the table with a pencil, "Now you're saying they have a fortress?"

"Had is the word" Sandy carried on, "They died out a few hundred years ago, but they did leave a couple of awesome fortresses, this one was their HQ, and the most formidable! But that's not why we're here"

"Okay" Jacko took the situation in. "So we've got an 'asset' possibly kidnapped and on the way to a medieval fortress, nothing out the ordinary then?" the irony wasn't lost on anyone. "Why?"

"Three years ago the fortress was bought by an organization using the name 'The Phoenix Foundation'" Sandy began.

"Like McGyver?" Joey asked, not quite knowing what to make of the situation.

"That WAS fiction you know" Sandy replied she was getting a little frustrated at Joey's seemingly trivial comments. She hadn't cottoned on that it was his way of dealing with stress, "But yes, the same name with little known about these folks. We do have a few leads on them, but basically, they seem to be 'guns for hire and to the highest bidder"

"What do we actually know about them then?" Jacko was getting a little impatient.

"Guns for hire to the highest bidder as I said" Sandy picked up from where she left off, "Mostly ex Spetznaz from the cold war era. And a few ex-Foreign Legion, they do have links to some unsavoury governments, hence the properties, and as far as we can tell Alamut may have been payment for services rendered training people Iran likes but doesn't want to be seen with"

"Now that's strange" The Colonel muttered, considering who we know the Iranians have been involved with in the past!"

"Not really!" It was Sir Michael interrupted this time, "Remember the Nukes deal with the U.S.? part of the deal was to put some distance between Iran and some of her previous friends, this" he gestured at the file on the table "Is Iran's way around it!" he looked directly at each one around the table and continued "We actually don't think Iran or the government there have anything to do with what's going on there so naturally, we'd like to keep them out of it!"

"In their fortress, in their country, probably surrounded by Republican Guard? Sure. No problem boss!" It was Mac with the jibe, though it wasn't lost on anyone. If Iran was dragged in it could turn a lot nastier than it already was.

"Soon as we're finished here your pilots will take us to Docklands," Sandy took back over the briefing "there's a 'civvie' plane waiting to fly us to Cyprus where a Hercules is scheduled to fly supplies to the Kurdish forces in Erbil, You'll happen to 'fall out the back of the plane over the mountains and HALO into Iran using wingsuits and chutes, from there you'll either extract or eliminate Chambers and return via the mountains back into Iraqi Kurdish territory" she stopped and made eye contact with all four men. A steely determination descended on the room, everyone there was determined that this was only going to end one way. Joey was smitten by Sandy but he was also totally focused on the job at hand, nothing was going to prevent the success of the mission.

It was the Colonel who broke the tension, "Gentlemen, this op is totally off the books!" he spoke slowly and seriously, "As of this moment you are no longer members of the SAS, papers are being drawn up with 'dishonourable discharges' for all of you, Should you be captured we can't help you! Do you understand that?"

No one spoke for a moment, not that they were needing to think about things, everyone knew the risks, "You mean 'The Secretary will disavow' us sir," Jacko spoke for all of them, each one nodding their heads. "No problem, Scorpion one's ready to sting!"

Chapter 2

"Good God I need a drink" Sir Michael was the one who spoke first after the team had left the room; he rose from his chair and headed for the door, opened it and turned to face Colonel Simpson. "Care to join me at my club Colonel?"

There was no need to ask why; it was obvious that Sir Michael hadn't told everything in the briefing, there was something he was keeping back. He was sending a team into harm's way, literally into the 'jaws of the lion' so to speak and he hadn't told them the whole story, what was going on?

"Sure" Colonel Simpson replied, "It's been a long and difficult day, would be nice to unwind a bit"

"Michelle" Sir Michael paged his secretary, "Can you have Stevens bring my car to the exit? Thanks so much" he clicked the intercom off; it was obvious he didn't want to say anything about the mission here.

Vauxhall house is about the most secure building in the United Kingdom, it's got every conceivable device for blocking phone tapping, parabolic mikes and every other eavesdropping device that's known to man, yet Sir Michael was willing to forego all those devices to tell him something, clearly, there was a problem!

The Mayfair club is the kind of place that never advertises for membership. It's the kind of place that you have to be invited by a member to join, not a 'closed club' as such but in many ways more secretive than the Masons, in fact, most of London's high society isn't even aware the club exists. A club totally for the 'elite' of the establishment and not even your father's membership can guarantee you getting invited to be a member. For the elite, protected by the elite.

Oak panelling from wall to wall greets you as you walk in the door, deep coloured carpeting giving a feeling of luxury and power, men sat quietly in corners sipping their gin and tonic, or Glenfiddich ten-year-old malt served by waiters dressed impeccably in full morning dress that looked as if they'd come straight from the drawing rooms of one of the great houses of the Victorian era waited on their every whim.

"Good evening Sir Michael" the doorman greeted them as soon as they walked in the door, "and welcome to our humble club Colonel Simpson, hope you enjoy your time here"

"Thank you Griffiths" Sir Michael replied as he handed his coat to the doorman, "Can you have the barman bring me my usual, and the Good Colonel will have?"

"Just an orange juice please" Colonel Simpson was somewhat thrown that the doorman, a man he'd never seen before knew his name. 'How the hell did he know who I was?'

"Don't worry about how Griffiths knew that" Sir Michael spoke quietly as they sat in a corner, "This club's got a better intelligence network than we have" he joked, "I'd be more worried if he didn't know who you were!"

Neither man spoke about the situation until the drinks had been served and the barman had retreated back to the bar.

"This whole bloody affair makes me sick!" it was a surprising statement from Sir Michael, "Sending people into danger with only half the picture"

"I gathered as much" Simpson replied, "What is it you're not telling them?"

"What's the chance they'll take the second option we gave them?"

"You mean the 'Kill' part?" Simpson replied in a matter of fact tone, "If you wanted that then you've got the wrong team! These boys are pretty good at choosing which orders they're going to obey!" he reached out and lifted the orange juice, swirling it around the glass as if it was a whiskey, "Hell itself will freeze over before they will even consider it"

"Part of me is glad to hear that. But part of me fears that might be their undoing!"

"But you chose the team personally, why the doubts now?"

"Chambers was working in a very small group" Sir Michael spoke in a low tone, "Outside of '6' no one knew what he was doing, that leaves the question how the bloody hell did the kidnappers know he'd be in the coffee house?"

"They could have gotten to the contact" Simpson suggested.

"That contact you talk about" Sir Michael carried on in the low tone "was a mid-level Lieutenant in the local drug gang, been feeding us and the yanks info for years." he shifted and reached for the Glenfiddich, "so that means there's a bloody leak somewhere! And as yet we don't know where"

"So" Colonel Simpson spoke slowly, "If there's a leak, then they know we'll be coming right?"

"And the tactics we'll possibly use"

"Now things make a bit more sense" Colonel Simpson scratched his head, "Jackson and his crew are about the most 'reliable' in some ways but yet the most 'unpredictable' in that they somehow, someway find a way to do what they promise in the way you least expect them to!"

"Any other team we send would probably just 'take the shot' when they get the chance" Sir Michael carried the thought on, "but Jackson and gang will probably try and break him out, and get killed in the process"

"Yet you're planning on them trying aren't you?" the Colonel slowed up as he spoke, he hated that Sir Michael had banked on the team taking a 'suicide mission' on without being given the whole story.

"Those four owe Chambers their lives after the last operation they were involved in"

"An op you wanted to pull the plug on as I recall" Simpson was still accusing.

"Chambers told me there and then, if I pull that plug then he'd damn well 'plug' me with his 9mm! Put the gun right in my damn face"

"So why are you even considering trying to get him out if it's a suicide mission?"

"Because if there is a leak" Sir Michael replied, "then Chambers knows who it is, and we need to find it fast, before it blows up in our face!" he stopped for a moment and reached for the whiskey glass, then slowly draining the glass he placed it back on the table and looked directly at Colonel Simpson. "But let me make one thing crystal clear Colonel, what I said over at 'the house' was for the benefit of the recording devices that are whirring over there, for the possible 'mole' to think that those men are out on a limb with no backup!"

"Are you saying?"

"That I've absolutely no bloody intention of abandoning them" he spoke slowly and deliberately, "They'll get Chambers out, and when they do I'm going to make damned sure that we get them out"

"But we're not sure where Chambers is are we?"

"He's already at the fortress" Sir Michael continued, "Cheltenham confirmed about ten minutes ago, I'm giving the go-ahead for Sandy to go in with the team and recover whatever intelligence we can get"

"Okay then" Simpson understood, "what do we need to do?"

"I need you in Syria" Sir Michael replied, "A visit to the troops or something when they contact us you'll need to do whatever it takes to get to them!" He handed the Colonel a manila envelope, it was obvious the old trickster had been planning this all along, "The Army Air Corps squadron supporting our troops fighting Isis has a flight with a Lynx and two 'Longbows' not doing much at the moment, the Pilots are pretty bored" he smiled as he said it, "I'm sure you've got a few things for them to do!

Chapter 3

"Fifteen minutes to Drop Zone" the pilot's voice came over their headsets; each one began their final checks. Joey checked the valve on his oxygen mask, skydivers jumped up to twelve thousand feet and occasionally went a little higher but Special Forces started training at that height, they'd be jumping at thirty-three thousand feet and that meant oxygen masks!

The whole of the first flight was spent checking the gear they'd brought in the bags, inspecting and cleaning weapons, making sure everything was as they were supposed to be. Every weapon the personal choice of the soldier or 'Blade' as the SAS like to be known, that is except for the dagger! Hence the nickname 'Blades'

Joey had his blade, a six-inch double bladed dagger, long, thin and deadly, superb balance made it as near perfect as it could be. He also carried a Browning 9mm as his sidearm but his main weapon was an M4 Colt commando with a thirty round magazine and underslung grenade launcher that had its own ten round magazine! Jacko had a bushmaster shotgun as well as the M4 but not the grenade launcher. Smithy had his Sako TRG sniper rifle with scopes for night and day work.

Naturally the change of plan hadn't been long after takeoff from Docklands so everyone had time to get used to it, clearly, the plan was 'on the fly' and could turn to shit real fast!

There were three, one Chambers was in Alamut so any action will be busting out of a medieval fortress, two was the destination of the plane, Kabul was the new destination with 'machine parts' so they could overfly Iran and get closer to the location. Three was Sandy was now going all the way with them! That meant that Joey was appointed as her 'guardian angel' with one job; make sure she makes it all the way!

Sandy was the one that probably had the hardest time with the change in plans. It took her a while to realize that the team seemed to just 'accept' that she'd be with them and that disturbed her somewhat.

"Aren't you worried about the change in plans?" she asked Jacko as soon as she got chance to speak with him on the plane.

"Not really" he replied almost in a 'matter of fact' tone, "We kind of expected a change, just not totally all he said"

"How did you know?"

"The stuff in the briefing room" Jacko replied. "We knew the info was true, at least what you were telling us, but we also knew Sir Mike was holding back!"

"But, aren't you worried?"

"Sandy" Jacko spoke softly so the others wouldn't hear, "You've been with MI6 how long? A couple of years"

"Just about" she replied annoyed that her inexperience showed up so much.

"What wasn't said in words" Jacko went on, "is that there's a mole, or at least Sir Michael thinks there is! And our job is to break Chambers out so he can tell us who that is"

He carried on. "What we didn't expect was that he'd send you in to get the extra intelligence, but that's his insurance policy in case we fail to get Chambers! It's also why I'm putting you and Joey together as a team"

Apparently the idea of breaking into a medieval fortress like this and getting a look at possible secrets that Phoenix might have was too good a chance to miss, and with the team already on the way, well that was just fine and dandy for the 'head shed' as the bosses in Whitehall were often called. "What the head shed wants, the head shed gets" was what Jacko often said, "And to hell with the consequences!"

"I don't bloody well need a nursemaid" she was furious when Jacko laid that condition down.

"Good! Because I'm not your nurse or a bloody maid!" Joey spoke up, "Now hold still while I adjust the straps" he was adjusting the fittings to the wingsuit and parachute.

"I don't damn well need your help" Sandy brushed his hands away and tried to reach the strap that needed adjustment.

"Listen lady" Joey was getting impatient, "You get those straps too loose, you'll end up with a broken arm or worse!" he pulled the straps hard, "Get them tangled and you won't need help. You'll need a coffin!" Sandy finally relented, though not without more protest, "Don't speak to me like that corporal!" She figured reminding him of his junior rank would put him in his place, as an MI6 operative she held the rank equal to a captain.

"Lady, you're in a Parachute harness" Joey shot straight back, "That makes it my turf! I'm the flamin' instructor, now do exactly as I say OK" that did not go down well he could see, but he really didn't give a shit, all he wanted was for the five of them to get down in one piece!

"Ten minutes to the DZ" the pilot's voice came over the intercom, "Stow all gear"

This was one trip where they were 'travelling light' but that still meant full combat gear along with pouches of ammunition (each one carrying at least two hundred rounds as well as thirty rounds each for the grenade launchers) enough to give the enemy a serious headache! What they weren't taking was the luxuries like food (eat what you kill or steal) apart from a few high energy bars each (ten per person, each with enough fuel stored to give you energy for the whole day and treated to give you constipation so you don't have to stop to take a dump! That way the enemy has less to track you with!

Jacko inspected each one making sure that nothing would rattle; even the slightest noise on the ground could get them some serious trouble and might get them killed.

"Five minutes" the voice came again, "open the cargo door." The loadmaster did one last check of the straps holding the pallets in place and then hooked his harness to the special seat he had and waited for the final thumbs up from Jacko.

They clipped their oxygen masks into place and gave the thumbs up to Jacko gave the signal to the loadmaster, He pressed the button and the back of the plane lowered revealing a cloudless sky thirty-five thousand feet over Iran, it was awesome, and scary for anyone who doesn't like heights and Sandy wasn't exactly fond of them.

"Don't look down' It was Joey's voice she heard in her headset, "Just look straight ahead and follow exactly what I say" for some reason right now she was glad for this big dumb Northerner who was actually taking the time to talk her through the jump, she'd never said anything about 'not liking heights' so there was nothing 'on file' yet he'd sensed it and stepped in.

"If we hold hands when we jump" he continued, "No one will notice, or care"

"Cheeky sod," She thought, "Is he trying it on, for God's sake!"

"Don't get the wrong idea!" he gently reminded her, apparently only the two of them were talking on this channel, "I'm trying to get you down in one piece, that's all"

H.A.L.O stands for High Altitude Low Opening and it's a specialty of the Military! Skydivers start freefall parachuting at 3,000 feet and go up as high as 12,000 normally because any higher and you need oxygen, but Special Forces often have to jump from high enough to pass off as civilian planes. They start training at 12,000 feet and keep going! 35,000 feet is a 'walk in the park' for them and shit scary for anyone else as they see the clouds literally miles below them!

"DZ in one minute" the voice came over. "Stand by!"

The red light by the door came on, it was activated by GPS telling them they were less than five miles from the target or Drop Zone (DZ) from now on everything was computer controlled and there was no turning back. The whole plane darkened as they approached the final point. Oxygen masks were turned on and visors lowered, each one reached around the back of the helmets and clicked a small switch that activated the night vision visors, everything turned green. The light turned amber but all they could see was that it was the second light in the panel, the last of the checks were carried out, they all stood Jacko and Mac first, Smithy next then came Joey with Sandy who was gripping so tight Joey thought he was losing circulation in his fingers!

The last light came on, it was Green for the loadmaster, but he was the only one could see it; he screamed "Green, Go, Go, Go" and they were away, stepping out into the night.

Chapter 4

His head hurt like hell, a migraine like he hadn't had since he was a kid. A piercing debilitating pain that just wouldn't let go no matter what was tried, not that his captors were going to give him anything for it. That was their plan or part of it, using the pain to 'soften him up' ready for when they start questioning what he knew.

It was all part of the 'technique' of softening up ready for interrogation that would come later, "Get the target to experience a few days of lack of sleep along with some pain and hunger and they'll tell you anything" was the theory, and to be honest it works ninety nine point nine percent of the time, but the point one percent, when it doesn't work, is when the person you're doing it on knows the technique and Chambers knew the technique as he'd used it himself at times.

The room had no windows, just four grey walls complimented with a grey floor and grey ceiling, the light was dim and the distinction between the two could hardly be seen, somewhere out there was the border between the floor and walls but he couldn't make it out at the moment.

All outside references had been removed from him, even the way of telling time. He had no concept of how long he'd been there, it could have been mere hours, or it could have been days or even weeks, there was just no way of knowing.

There was a door! It looked old but sturdy, and it did have one modern piece of equipment, a spy hole in the door, he couldn't see out of the spy hole but they could see in! And with it they were keeping an eye on him.

There was a wooden bench at the far end of the room, a dirty bench that he wouldn't normally even sit on with a thick blanket or newspapers between him and the bench, but he didn't have the newspapers and the floor was even worse in some ways, rat droppings covered parts of the floor, he just couldn't see where the rats were or where they came from, but the droppings looked fresh.

"God, this bloody head hurts" he talked to himself. They say that the first sign of madness is talking to yourself, but when you've no one else to talk to who else can you talk to? 'Besides, they're listening' he thought and if they're listening then are you really 'talking to yourself' or giving your captors feedback as to how well their technique was working? He decided to 'lead them up the garden path' and start the 'game of cat and mouse' that was real interrogation, they'd not find this easy!

It was very much a game of 'cat and mouse' he knew and unfortunately he was the mouse in the jaws of a very nasty and hungry cat and he knew it.

He looked at the plate that had been passed through the small hatch in the door, it had a small piece of stale black bread and a half a cup of lukewarm water, each bit was designed to break him in the fastest possible way and to be honest, it didn't really matter that he knew that, the things they were doing would do their work anyway, it's just that it would take a little longer!

The stale bread did tell him something though, it told him that he wasn't a prisoner of any Middle Eastern outfit, they didn't eat black bread! They would have used stale pita bread, the Egyptians would have used wholemeal pita where the Lebanese and Syrians would have used white bread and the Iranians would have used bread more like the Indian naan bread. That meant the people who had him were probably Eastern European or maybe even Russian!

But he still had no idea where he was! And he had no idea if London knew where he was, let alone whether they could get him out?

"Getting out' the thought brought a smile to his face, you have to hold out hope in these situations, and he knew they'd be 'burning the midnight oil' to try and find him, hopefully if the tracker in his shoulder was still working then they might have an idea where he was, he couldn't feel any wound so that suggested that his captors didn't know about it, but he had noticed a few teeth missing, and that added to the pain he was feeling, it's just "A bloody headache" was so much worse than a few missing teeth that had been removed without any anaesthetic! No, he was going nowhere anytime soon.

He headed for the bench shuffling across the floor as best he could, the chains around his legs restricting his movement, that's when he noticed the chains were attached to the wall and he just about reached the bench when they drew tight, even that was going to be denied him! The bench being there was part of the mental torture, he tried to shut the world out, tried to close his eyes and imagine that he was home in Ankara with his wife and family, He'd been such a bloody fool the morning he'd left and they'd had an argument over the stupidest of things, but then again hindsight is always twenty-twenty isn't it? Now, unless a miracle happened he'd not get the chance to say sorry!

He closed his eyes, they'd been closed for a few moments when the intensity of the light increased dramatically, he stayed with his eyes closed, they hurt and he needed to rest. A few minutes later, just as he was getting used to the light the noise came on, someone must have a sick sense of humour as it was the bagpipes being played out of tune (if you could) and they sounded horrendous, he couldn't even make out the tune they were trying to play, it was just loud annoying noise!

At other times they'd used 'white noise' which was just static playing very loudly with no rhyme or anything, just to keep him awake and on edge, when that didn't work, well he'd found out that there was a sprinkler system installed in the cell and freezing cold water came down through the system, either that or boiling hot water depending on how sadistic the operator was!

The walls were stone, cold and wet. That made him wonder if he was underground somewhere, the cold stone indicated that the walls were old; possibly some old ruins that some big outfit had bought and were using for their own means, or maybe they were squatting and no one knew they were here.

This area of the world was literally covered with old ruins that no one used any longer, everything from old places thousands of years old to the more recent medieval forts that dotted the skyline, even Saddam had built hundreds of secret police forts on the top of just about every mountain all with the purpose of intimidating the locals, none of this helped him work out where he was or whether the tracker would work under so much stone!

'Not exactly the Hilton!' was all he could think.

Chapter 5

The freefall took fifteen minutes. Fifteen minutes of brutal temperatures (minus fifty with wind-chill taking it down to minus sixty or more). Fifteen terrifying but exhilarating minutes. Sandy was scared out of her wits, yet at the same time loving every minute of it!

She knew that if she hit the ground without the 'chute' she would be killed so quickly that she probably wouldn't feel a thing, yet she'd be conscious all the way down and certain of the outcome. Yet from so far up it was like floating in a starlit sky, literally 'falling from the heavens'

"Keep your arms out like in the surrender position" It was Joey's voice over the radio; they had a channel for him to talk her down as none of the others were monitoring this frequency. He was frustrating at times and talked as if she was some little schoolgirl who knew nothing, but at the same time, she was kind of getting used to the 'big oaf' with his 'big brother' attitude.

"Keep the arms in that position" Joey was saying, "That'll keep you balanced and stop you spiralling all over the sky and we pull the chord at five thousand!"

'Roger that big brother' she felt like saying, but what came out was "OK got that" he was only a couple of months older than her, and she'd done a skydive before, but this was nuts, diving from thirty-five thousand feet into mountains AT NIGHT and on top of that they're using the wingsuits to glide to the place they want to be, but with no Landing zone marked on the ground. She'd heard that to be a paratrooper you had to have a lobotomy, now she believed it!

They had altimeters fitted to the suits that worked off air pressure, they'd been set for sea level to give an accurate reading of the altitude so that they knew when to pull the cords, the ground was at four thousand feet so pulling at five thousand would give a couple of minutes to slow the descent and get their bearings.

The 'rip cord' was on her right-hand side so as she passed six thousand one hundred feet she extended her right arm above her head and reached across with the left, taking hold of the chord she gave it a hard tug and for the first second nothing happened.

Terror struck, 'the damn thing's not working, ROMAN CANDLE' was the immediate thought she opened her mouth to scream but it was cut short as she was slammed into the harness with such force it took her breath away. Decelerating from 120 feet per second to five feet per second almost instantly does that to you! The relief was amazing. Reaching up for the controls she began to maneuver the parachute so that she was following the others.

Joey's chute opened next, then Smithy, Mac and finally Jacko pulled his cord as he passed eight hundred feet, it wasn't bravado that made him pull so late, but needing to clear the other chutes first, besides in an operational HALO they often get as low as four hundred feet first, it's just that in the mountains they'd erred on the side of caution.

"Landing Zone's on our left" Jacko advised through the headset, "Follow me" and with that, he started drifting into a wide turn and lining up with the only level piece of ground they could see.

The Night vision visors they were using allowed for full 180-degree vision and were capable of making a starlit night look like broad daylight, it just looked like a 'green day'. They worked by taking the starlight and magnifying it so that you could see everything, only trouble was they chewed up battery power and would need recharging during the day as the solar batteries only lasted a few hours.

Reaching back across with her left hand she disconnected her oxygen supply and opened the valve that allowed her to breathe normally while still wearing the mask, Joey wanted the oxygen tanks with as much oxygen in he'd told them and she could only guess why she chose not to!

Just before his feet touched 'terra firma' she saw Jacko 'flare the chute' and literally just begin walking, he literally walked to his landing! She saw each of the team do the same thing and it was stunning, she did the same and apart from a bit of a heavy landing she came down totally in control of the descent and was stunned to realize she was still upright!

The moment they were down the team took the chutes off and deployed into a defensive position, they'd parachuted with magazines on the weapons but nothing in the chamber, all that changed as each one silently cocked their weapons, safeties stayed on though.

"All yours Joey" was all Jacko said and Joey immediately moved out of the perimeter and began working packing the chutes away, Jacko powered down his Night vision visor and waited. "Sandy" he spoke softly over the headset, "Help Joey"

It takes twenty minutes for the human eye to adjust to the dark, take that time without any light and you'd be stunned at what you can see! As her eyes adjusted it was as if she'd never seen the sky so clear before, every star was so bright, even trees in the distance could be seen, she could see the outline of each of the four men with her and what they were doing, apart from Joey' they were all silently watching, totally motionless blending in with the background, waiting to see what shouldn't be there.

The chutes were packed away, Joey gave each chute back to its owner, nothing could be left behind, there had to be no trace they'd ever been here. Joey and Sandy rejoined the team in the perimeter, they'd powered down their visors as well.

"Three hours to sunrise" Jacko whispered, "twenty-five miles to the target, we'll make ten before sunrise and wait out the day." The plan had been for a three-day hike to the fortress, it was still the plan! Rising from his kneel he whispered "Let's move"

Chapter 6

Slowly each of the team rose and set off, Smithy, as the keenest eyes and the team sniper had 'point' and the responsibility of watching the arc ahead of them to make sure they didn't get any nasty surprises coming from the 11 o'clock to 2 o'clock position. Jacko was next, they'd agreed before setting out where the first 'RV' was. It was a mountain ridge they could see in the moonlight, Jacko was about three metres behind and to two to the right of Smithy; he had the 8 o'clock to 11 o'clock to watch.

Behind and to the left was Mac with the 2 o'clock to 5 o'clock to watch, finally Joey had the 'tail end Charlie' job of watching everyone's backs, he spent most of the time actually walking backwards making sure no one gave them any nasty surprises from behind, Sandy was given the job of walking level with Joey but off to one side and making sure there was nothing he was going to trip over when walking backwards.

Ten miles in three hours would be easy during daylight on a level road, but it wasn't daytime and where they were wasn't flat! The patch of ground was flat, but in the direction they were heading the mountains rose up either side as they walked along the floor of a small valley. Just to the right, they could hear flowing water that seemed to be getting louder every few hundred metres, clearly, the river cut across their path at some point.

Smithy stopped dead and slowly descended to the kneeling position, he'd seen something or someone. In total silence the team all did the same, everyone watching their designated 'arc' and keeping an eye on Smithy for his next move.

No hand signals were given yet each of the team knew exactly what to do next, it came from many months working together, learning how each member of the team thinks. Smithy was fully prone now and extending the bipod on the sniper rifle watching for trouble. Jacko had moved forward and was scanning the area with Binoculars; it was a red light he'd seen, probably from a cigarette about two hundred metres away straight ahead.

Whoever it was wasn't going to be friendly. 'Could be Shepherds' they pretty much all thought, but then where were the sheep? 'More likely smugglers of some kind' was the next thought; the team had no intention of finding out!

Jacko signalled the rest of the team to head off on a tangent, Mac, Joey and Sandy headed that direction and as soon as they got level with the man smoking they stopped, then went to ground, there were three of them but far enough away that the team could move carefully without being seen. One quick click of the mike told Jacko and Smithy to join them, everyone watched their arc's despite the temptation to all watch the drowsy men who eventually stubbed out their cigarette and went off the sleep blissfully unaware of how close to a silent but violent end they'd come.

About a mile further on they came to the source of the noise of the running water, a small river flowing over rocks. It wasn't deep, just up to their waists but at thirty feet wide it wasn't that easy to cross either.

They'd taken up a defensive position again while Jacko surveyed the situation, as soon as that was done he and Mac took the ropes they were all carrying, tied them together and threaded one end around a tree, Stripping everything off right down to his underwear Mac put all his clothes and equipment into a plastic bag which he then put into his backpack. The stuff that wouldn't fit there like his weapons and boots he attached to its sides (in other plastic bags) then he took both ends of the rope and tied them around his waist before wading the river, the pack and rifle were left on the bank for the boys to attach to the rope and arrange to ferry across later.

As soon as he was across the river he found a suitable tree and looped the ropes around it then started pulling knowing that team would see the rope moving and start attaching the packs so that he could get them across on a sort of pulley system. Within minutes he was joined by Smithy and Jacko who'd waded the river and worked the system. They'd literally walked under the packs making sure everything got over without getting wet and brought Mac's equipment with them, as soon as they were there they quickly changed back into their combat gear and took up defensive positions to make sure Joey and Sandy who'd stayed behind to make sure they were 'covered' could make the crossing safely, they brought up the rear of the unit.

The weapons they carried had clips fitted that enabled them to be clipped to the combat webbing for the parachute jump so they could make a freefall with their weapons attached and have no issues. The team clipped the weapons, webbing and backpacks all together then used the slings of the weaponry to attach the bundle to the ropes.

There were two things that they could not afford to get wet, one was the ammunition, water seeping into a round of ammunition, even just one could get you killed in a firefight as your weapon 'misfired' but your opposition firing that tenth of a second later (and a tenth of a second before you could eject the round and get a new hopefully dry one) means a body bag for you! The second was the electronic equipment they were carrying including small portable solar panels for recharging the night vision visors and Sandy's Satellite phone.

As soon as they were all across, Mac and Jacko untied the rope ends then started pulling one end. As each piece came across the ropes were untied from the longer one, checked and rewound ready for the next time, even Sandy had stripped down to her underwear, they each got re-dressed, in turn, making sure that the group was fully protected at all times.

"We're behind schedule boss!" Mac spoke in a low voice, "No way will we make ten before sunrise!"

"Shit happens" Jacko replied in as low a voice. "We'll still make eight, that'll have to be enough for now!" rising from his crouch he spoke softly "OK folks, let's get moving again"

The day starts in Iran with a call from the minaret, the call to prayer given. The 'Fajr' prayer is the most important as it's when people start moving around, tradition has it that it's when the Angels change their guard and those who've guarded the night go back to heaven while the new guards of the day take over, the team could hear the call to prayer in the village far away, they also knew that it's about the time any shepherds would be waking up.

They were high in the mountains now, finding a small valley where a small stream had once come crashing down, the rocks looked as if in winter and spring the stream might return with a force, but right now, at the beginning of the autumn the bed was dry and gave good cover from the rest of the valley. Halfway up the valley Smithy stopped, everyone immediately went to ground. The sun was just beginning to show, its first slivers touching the horizon as it rose.

Jacko went forward at Smithy's signal, within minutes he was signalling them forward, they spotted a cave that would be great for what they need.

The one advantage of caves over camping is they are always cool, the sun almost never gets to the back of most caves, so they stay cool, even when the temperatures are hitting 120 degrees in the shade a cave will be a cool 50 or so degrees.

The entrance was pretty narrow, just wide enough for one to squeeze through at a time that was both good and bad! Good in that they'd be able to guard it pretty easily, but bad in that if it was the only way in then if an enemy showed up they'd be trapped and would need to fight their way out.

"Mac" Jacko spoke to the big Scotsman as he passed into the cave, "Check for any exits at the back, you know what we need." That was simple if he found one he was to rig a warning device so that anyone coming that way doesn't stumble into a squad of unprepared Special Forces who weren't meant to be there. The rest of the team began unpacking their equipment and cleaning their weapons.

There's an order to things in situations like this that must be followed at all times, your life literally 'hangs in the balance' miss one out or get it wrong and it could kill you! The first priority is always clean and check your weapons make sure they're 100% 'good to go' and when you need them they will be! Number two is food! Eat what you need to eat, but don't bloat yourself! 'Blades' know what they need and are clued up on nutrition so they get what they need and no more. Number three is sleep, once the other two are done, if you've no work then get some sleep as you don't know when you're going to get the next opportunity, it could be days away.

Mac took about fifteen minutes to sort out the rear, "There's an entrance there, goes in about three hundred feet, and then cuts up. Comes out on the other side of the ridge about a hundred feet from the top"

"Sounds like a good route for an emergency!" Jacko replied. "We've sorted out three-hour stints for guard duty" He explained. "It's 7 am now, Joey and Sandy will take the first, then me, then Smithy and finally you've got from 4 to 7 pm!"

"Sounds good to me" Mac replied and immediately grabbed his pack, they'd passed an orchard on the way and 'liberated' a few of the apples that had fallen from the trees, being slightly bruised no one would really notice them missing, and with the energy bars they'd give that little bit more energy for the following day. He tucked into an apple as he laid out the groundsheet for sleeping, within minutes those not guarding had finished their apples and energy bars and were asleep.

The Army says the most likely time for an attack is either just before dawn or just after sunset as that's the time when folks are the most vulnerable, in the morning they're still waking up and at night the eyes haven't totally adjusted to the lack of light (and the fact people want to sleep) so it's a standard practice for all military units within the British Army to 'Stand to' for an hour just before dawn and just about sunset, the Regiment is the same! The team was 'stood to' weapons at the ready from 7 pm until about an hour after dark; it was 8.30 when Jacko called the team together for a briefing.

It was more like a 'brainstorm than a briefing! Regular units have their officers get up and tell the men the great life-saving plans they've come up with, the Regiment knows better and everyone gets a say in the plan.

"We should arrive just before dawn" Jacko looked around the group, four tense faces looked at the map he'd spread out in front of them.

They ran through all the preparations they could think of at the time and tried to work them out ahead of time but in the end, they were agreed that 'fine tuning' the plan would have to wait until they got there.

"Right then" Jacko stood up and looked around the team, "Lead us off Smithy".

Chapter 7

The first glimpse of the fortress was when they exited the cave, in the twilight they could see lights high on the mountains to the East, too high up for it to be a village. It had to be Alamut. The light was like a beacon calling to them 'come closer' and like moths to a flame, they were drawn towards that light.

Just before the dawn began to break Jacko called a halt in a small wood halfway up the mountain, there was a small dried up river bed running into the wood from the left, it seemed to originate further up near the other peak, "If we head up the river bed we should be able to stay out of sight of the fortress" he spoke quietly, "That way hopefully we're not seen"

"What about villagers?" Sandy asked none of them wanted to be detected so close to the target. The last thing they needed was some villager strolling into their camp and setting off the alarm!

"We're pretty close to the snow line" Jacko replied, "any shepherds or other people with the right to be out will be further down the mountain.

"Don't forget smugglers!" Sandy replied. "What about them?"

"We're off the main smuggling route here" it was Joey who replied, kind of surprising Sandy a bit, "and it's unlikely they'll want smugglers so close to their own base, there might be a patrol, but even that's unlikely"

Being such a remote location can have its advantages and one of them is it's easy to keep an eye on what's going on around you. Putting checkpoints out on the roads and the occasional patrol through the valley would be enough to deter the villagers from prying too much, anything else and if the Iranians found out about armed guards patrolling mountains could cause more trouble than it's worth.

"They'll be pretty vigilant in the fortress" Mac spoke up, "with sentries etc, but probably confident they can stop anything without needing to blanket the bloody place"

Smithy was the first to go. He advanced about a hundred meters then went to ground and called the next forward. At all times one was moving, but the other four were watching ready to let hell itself loose if they were seen. The going was slow, but by two hours after dawn they were close to where they wanted to be for the observation point; there they'd be able to watch the fortress for the next thirty-six hours.

In any engagement or firefight the key is always how good your intelligence is. Get that wrong and you could go thinking you're facing a 'washed up bunch of old farts and schoolboys' but end up staring down two divisions of the best the enemy has to offer, most of the team were from the Parachute Regiment and the lessons of Arnhem have not been forgotten! Intel would be the key here too, especially when they'd no idea how many were in the fortress.

Sandy also had a Sat phone (Satellite phone) that didn't need a mobile network as it transmitted directly to satellites overhead and could send and receive encrypted messages, they'd been careful not to use it as they knew the Iranians and the Americans would pick up the signal, but the agreement was one message when they got into position, a short 'microburst' lasting about one hundredth of a second that would tell London all they need to know, then 24 hours later they'd get one back with the latest intelligence reports on the fortress and Phoenix they might need to know. She took the phone out of her pack, pulled out the antennae and punched in a four-digit code. Joey watched and took note of the code. As soon as the code was punched in she put the antennae down.

"Don't you need to report in?" Joey asked.

"Just did" Sandy replied, "All they need to know is we're here and the missions on schedule!"

"Don't they need to know how or anything?"

"The less London knows about how the better it is for us." She replied, clearly there was stuff London wasn't telling the team, and maybe stuff Sir Michael wasn't telling London! "Besides, we don't need to report in again for another 24 hours, and then we'll get what London knows about the inhabitants"

The Observation Post or 'O.P.' was a couple of boulders that had fallen down the slope in a landslide at some time in the past, just behind the rocks there was a slight ledge and a path leading away around the side of the mountain. The path lead to a small clump of trees hidden from the fortress, the trees had wild berries growing along with what looked like a couple of apple trees and a walnut tree, there were apples on the trees but it didn't look as if they were tended. Joey started to forage a little around the clearing for whatever he could find.

Smithy had the job of building a shelter at the 'O.P.'. As the unit sniper he was the one going to be manning this place during the assault, giving cover and support to the rest of the unit, so he was put in charge of building the shelter and making sure it couldn't be seen.

The two boulders had a small opening at the base that one man could just crawl through; the ledge was about a foot in front of that. Taking out his groundsheet he laid it out flat at the front of the boulders.

The sheet had metal rings at the edges; the rings themselves were painted matt green just like the rest of the sheet. He took out a couple of plastic tent pegs and drove them into the ground, they were pretty strong so he didn't need to be gentle, and being so remote he took the risk and using a couple of rocks he drove the pegs hard into the ground.

Next he lifted the groundsheet using a few sticks he'd found in the clearing, using two sticks at the front and two at the back about three feet apart he was able to raise the groundsheet and give clearance enough for one to fit comfortably in the position, he'd need the extra room for his kit once the rest of the team moved out ready for the assault.

The art of good camouflage is blending in with your surroundings, using the groundsheet meant that he could deploy the rifle and the telescopic sights without fear of being seen, the key to that was that the sight itself would be at least a foot back out of the sun, the worst thing they could have now would be the inhabitants of the fortress realizing they were being watched by seeing the sun reflecting off a gun sight! Setting the sights back in the shade avoided that possibility.

Most amateurs make the mistake of putting the rifle so that the muzzle peeks out into the sunlight, do that and you can almost guarantee that if you're facing the wrong way the sun is going to reflect off the scope and it's like sending the enemy a text with your coordinates! The best way to combat it is simply set things about a foot or so back into the shade, that means you can see, but you can't be seen!

When everything was set up he got a couple of reasonably sized rocks and put them near the front of the shelter, but far enough back that nothing would be seen 'protruding' from the front, not even the muzzle of the rifle. Nothing gives away a position more than a straight line where they shouldn't be, and there are no straight lines in nature! A straight stick protruding from a rock just screams 'SNIPER' and when that happens you can guarantee the only one dying that day is the sniper and not the target!

Now it was time to settle in for the watching, he took a notebook and pencil out of his pocket and set them down, from now on everything coming and going from the fortress would be noted on one page while at the same time on one of the others he'd draw out a rough sketch of the fortress with the positions of each and every person noted.

Two vehicles moved up the mountain. From the way they moved Smithy could tell they were armoured, the extra weight and noise of the engine was the giveaway! Two Toyota Landcruisers with 4.5-litre engines, good four-wheel drive vehicles almost as robust as the Humvee loved so much by the US military, over here the Landcruiser was so common that virtually everyone had them, they were also ideal for the terrain.

Sentries patrolled the top of the ramparts, he could make out at least five sentries at the front with another half dozen or so scattered round the perimeter of the fortress, each one seemed to have their own area to patrol, he was particularly interested in the Western side.

The fortress itself sits on a rock outcrop, with the ridge running south before climbing to their position. On the West, the ground drops sharply away from the road so that by the time you get to the North wall you've got a fifteen hundred foot sheer drop that gets even further as you get to the Eastern side, right at the Northeast corner it's actually more like two thousand feet straight down.

Coming further round the rock quickly comes back up to meet the road, though the whole ridge is actually a ledge with the last part a six hundred foot climb straight up a sheer rock face. "Not an easy climb" was his words, but thinking, 'Thank God I don't have to!'

Towards the back of the compound, he could see radio antennae indicating where the command post was, it had a flat roof that looked like it had a 'H' painted there, just as he noted it he heard the familiar sound of rotors approaching.

"Smithy" a voice spoke up from behind the rocks, it was Jacko coming for a look himself, "what's approaching?" he was worried what the approaching sound meant, air support for the fortress!

"You're not going to like this boss" Smithy's reply was quiet but to the point, "A bleedin' Hind A just showed up!! It's in Gazprom markings too!!"

"SHIT! You gotta be kidding me!" Jacko's frustration was obvious. The Hind A is one of the deadliest Helicopters ever to take to the skies! Carrying a thirty millimetre cannon in the nose, two side mounted machine guns and when the rocket pods are fitted over a hundred and sixty 'fire and forget' rockets that can open a Tank like a tin opener opens a tin of beans, then there are the eight fully armed troops it can carry at the same time! Not a beast you want to argue with. Even the Apaches can't match that firepower, and one was landing at Alamut!!

"Keep an eye on it" Jacko spoke as much to regain control as anything else, "If it's still there when we go in we'll just have to deal with it and can't have them using that in a pursuit!"

"Will do boss"

Jacko turned to Sandy who was not far behind, "What the hell are Gazprom doing here? And what the bloody hell are they doing with a flamin' Hind? I thought they didn't sell to civilian outfits?"

"They have a pipeline into Central Asia not too far away, it goes all the way out from here and into Eastern Turkey" She replied, "They're also building a pipeline all the way down to the Persian Gulf so they can ship out through there too! In case we try and impose sanctions again! And just because the paintwork says 'civilian doesn't mean a thing! Question is how much are the Iranians in on it?"

"And Phoenix just happen to be their 'security people'?" he asked with a note of sarcasm "Would have been nice to know before" he wasn't angry, not with Sandy at least, but frustrated would be too mild a way of saying it!

"Didn't know until the 'Hind' showed up" Sandy replied, and it was partly true, she didn't know, but she couldn't answer for all MI6

Chapter 8

The rest of the day was spent either eating or sleeping if you weren't on duty that was. Joey and Sandy had foraged some food, wild carrots and onions that Joey had managed to turn into a 'passable' soup of some kind, then again after nearly two days without much food even boiled veggies can feel like a 'Gourmet meal'

As soon as the food was eaten everyone went to sleep except the one manning the O.P. which was changed every three hours so that everyone got a decent rest, they'd need it for the task ahead.

The Hind was at the fortress for most of the day but left about two hours before the twilight, she was last seen climbing and heading for Tehran, the team were still none the wiser how Gazprom was tied to this whole mess! The Hind herself didn't seem to be carrying rocket pods but they couldn't be sure about the canon!

By late afternoon everyone was rested, at least as rested as could be, Jacko sent Sandy to man the O.P. for the last couple of hours while the last preparations for the final ascent and assault on the fortress were made.

The plan had a simple beginning, but having to take Sandy along to gather intelligence had complicated matters somewhat. Sandy was pretty tough, and the lads all appreciated her, but she was no soldier and the next part demanded not just fitness but ruthlessness that civilians seldom possess! They needed to plan it out down to the last detail.

"What's the latest from the fortress?" Jacko began the 'open forum' type briefing, they were sitting around in a semi-circle at the back of the makeshift camp, even though Sandy wasn't there she was within hearing distance and could hear everything they were saying, but that was OK with everyone as they weren't trying to hide anything, it was just they needed to plan everything down to the last detail. They'd each spent some time at the O.P. but it was Smithy had the notebook, he took over.

"Looks like we're up against between forty to forty five hostiles" Smithy began, "That's what we've seen on the battlements, then we've got possibly ten or so running their coms centre!" he looked round the group expecting questions, "That's on site, off site we've got the Hind and however many she can bring, possibly about eight at a time"

Jacko interrupted there with news about the Hind, "Apparently she's a military surplus buy from the Russian military about three years ago, they bought four of them to patrol the pipeline they're building from Siberia through to Turkey, the other three are deployed further up the line near the Chinese border" he shifted slightly, stretching his legs out a little, "The pipeline's about a thousand miles long and the other three are stationed and pretty equal distances, the nearest other is two hundred miles away"

"Where's this one based?" Mac asked the obvious question everyone wanted to know and hoped it was as far away as possible.

"Nearest airfield capable of handling the Hind is 'Khomeini international' just outside Tehran" Jacko replied. "Gazprom has a hangar there in the industrial part"

"So they're about half an hour away from air support?" it was Mac who asked the question.

"Seems that way" Jacko replied, "Smithy, lay out the fortress for us" he looked directly at Smithy bringing the briefing back to its primary task and handing it over the Smithy.

"Four sentry posts at the front of the fortress" he began, "all manned twenty-four seven with at least one man" he took his notebook out of his pocket and began drawing a rough diagram in the dirt with a stick, "Here, here, here and here. The rest of the fortress is patrolled by roving guards, they're meant to be random but seem to be lazy and follow a pattern, and here it is" he drew the diagram showing the patrol pattern. "Roughly five minutes between patrols"

"So, we've got lazy guards round the back," Joey spoke up. "Probably confident they're so remote there's no chance of any nasty surprises; what about the front? How often are they swapped in the guard towers?"

"From what we saw" Smithy came back with a reply "Every three hours they change and the guards doing the patrolling go into the towers while the guards in the towers patrol the rest of the grounds. Every twelve hours there's a complete change of the guards"

"What about the helicopter?" Mac asked, "How does that fit in the picture?"

"As far as I can see" Smithy replied "They're using it to rotate the guard units, a new one every day is my guess"

"Which means they've got backup at Khomeini international" Joey interrupted. "An hour away"

"Yep, but they can only get a team of eight here each time! And that takes about 45 minutes flying time"

"What about vehicles?" Jacko asked.

"Six counted" Smithy replied, "five look like Landcruisers and one Eva truck, ex-East German Army!"

The briefing continued as the team discussed the entry point and how they were going to get out of the fortress.

The truth was Jacko wasn't all that happy with one piece of news that he had to give, disturbing news that London had delivered. GCHQ had picked up 'chatter' on the networks, Phoenix was making promises that meant only one thing, they were 'moving the heavies in' and it had to be tonight!

"We go tonight boys," Jacko said, "We've two hours to sunset, we move out in half an hour"

Chapter 9

They reached their 'staging point' just as the last rays of sunlight were disappearing. They made their last minute preparations and checked all their equipment, the weapons were all checked, all magazines were full, but nothing in the 'chamber'.

"Scorpion three this is Scorpion one" Jacko spoke softly into his headset mike, "Sierra Papa in five over". He let Smithy know they were moving out from the staging point in five minutes; Smithy began a final scan of the area making sure there were no nasty surprises.

"One this is three" Smithy came back over the radio, he was still at the 'O.P' as that's where he was needed during the assault, he'd be covering team's entry into the fortress and 'talking them through' where the enemy were, his job was to make sure they weren't detected as they made entry and to give 'covering support' for Jacko and Mac as they brought Chambers out, "You're good to go"

Jacko turned to Joey, as the most experienced mountaineer in the team Joey had been given the role of leading this part of the assault. He took up a position at the head "We should be good scrambling up this part boss" he observed, the terrain was steep, but not too tricky.

The fortress was five hundred feet above them, the first three hundred feet would be a relatively easy 'scramble' up the mountain, and they expected it to take just a few minutes. The second part was a different story.

Two hundred feet of a steep cliff face, not without handholds, but not something to be taken lightly, the idea was to stop and wait until it was completely dark with the moon out for that part of the climb.

As soon as it was dark enough they activated their night vision visors on the helmets and they were away, the green light helping them see as if it was day, twenty minutes later they'd cleared the first part of the climb and took a couple of minutes break ready for the hard part.

"Wait until I get to the top," Joey told the rest as he began the climb, the going was pretty easy using the night vision visor but the important part wasn't the climb so much as making sure that no one in the fortress heard them coming. There was still plenty of activity in the fortress, but it was all inside and near the front of the buildings, Smithy was keeping an eye on them.

"Four hold" Smithy's voice came over with a sense of urgency just as Joey was about to climb over the top of the cliff, he froze. "Bandit passing you" Smithy spoke again, 'Bandit was the code they were using for an enemy. "You're clear now, should have ten minutes" he spoke again.

Joey literally jumped over the top of the cliff, there was a ledge about four feet wide between it and the walls of the fortress. A small bush was growing just there. Taking the rope from off his shoulder he tied one end round his waist and wrapping it round the bush he gently and silently lowered the other end down the cliff, the idea was that the next person would tie the rope round their waist and begin to climb, Joey would keep the rope tight (but not pull too hard) and give the person extra stability by holding them with a 'fifth' anchor point thus allowing them to move that little bit quicker.

Sandy was the next over the top, she took ten minutes where Joey had taken twenty, as soon as she was over the top they heard Smithy say "Our friendly bandit's back, they laid prone next to the bush and just waited.

"You're clear" Smithy came over the mike, Sandy untied herself and moved further along the wall, towards the northern end, she found a rock and melded herself to its contours. Jacko and Mac followed in the next twenty minutes Joey moved off as soon as Jacko was up and got ready for scaling the walls.

Climbing the walls was pretty easy compared to the cliffs, there were places where the rocks had worn and toe and handholds could be had, it took him a couple of minutes but he was soon in the fortress.

It was the smell that gave the sentry away, Joey could smell the tobacco, cheap Turkish tobacco. There was a low table like object nearby so he crouched down behind it, "Where is he Smithy?" he spoke softly into the mike.

"About twenty feet away, just about to come round the corner" Smithy's reply was almost as quiet. Joey tensed up, every sense going into overdrive, he was upwind of the target which gave him all the advantages, silently he slipped his knife out of its sheath and readied himself. "He's mine" Joey spoke again.

"Roger that" Smithy replied.

The sentry was totally oblivious to the impending danger, more intent on enjoying the cigarette he was 'just going through the motions' of guarding the base, secure in the thought that nothing and no one could get to them! How wrong could he be?

He drew level with Joey, but was focused more on the cigarette than looking anywhere, not even taking a moment to check the valley below or enjoy the star-filled sky; Joey slowly raised himself to his full height, then silently took two steps forward into action.

A hand shot round the sentries' mouth, a cry of terror welling up within, he opened his mouth to scream and raised his arms to break the hold, but nothing happened as a sharp pain at the base of his skull was all he felt as the knife entered the neck, severing the spinal column right between the brainstem and the first vertebrae.

All feeling was lost and the heart stopped, the lungs no longer functioned as their communication path with the brain was severed, not even the voice box would function as the sentry couldn't exhale or get the air to pass through it! The body was already dead, only the facial muscles, the eyes and the tear glands continued to respond to the brain's commands.

Joey gently laid the man down, more because of not wanting to alert other sentries with noise than any sense of mercy; he quickly stripped the man of all his weapons, the AK47 Sandy could use, but the grenades he had a use for. Next, he removed the man's jacket and boots, Chambers would need them.

The rest of the team were waiting at the base of the walls, they'd heard the exchange between Joey and Smithy but knew nothing of the outcome. The next thing they knew was when the body silently came flying over the wall and crashed down beside them. Jacko and Mac stepped up rolling the man over the cliff and into the abyss.

"We're clear" Joey spoke again. "Up you come folks"

Jacko and Mac came before Sandy, as soon as they were in Joey heard a faint 'click' as they clicked their silencers onto their sidearms, then stealthily they moved off towards the keep.

Every Medieval fortress has a keep, a stronghold where the defenders could retreat to as a last resort if the outer walls of the fortress were breached, a place to wait it out until relief came or as a 'last stand' as the leadership negotiated terms for surrender. The keep was about thirty feet by forty-five feet. It stood three storeys tall.

The satellite dishes on the roof would have given things away, the top floor of the keep was traditionally the abode of the 'Lord of the Manor', this was being used as the Command and control centre, the next two levels would be the accommodation block and the 'cellar' underground was always where the Dungeon was, that was where Chambers was almost certainly being kept.

As soon as they were with him they took out their sidearms and gently clicked their silencers into place, all Joey heard was a very slight click.

"When Sandy gets here, give us two minutes" Jacko whispered into his mike, "Shouldn't need longer than that" and with that, they both moved off in the direction of the keep.

It was in the Northeast corner of the fortress with one door entering it from the battlements into the Command centre, they could see lights on.

Sandy pulled herself over the battlements and made ready to follow Jacko, Joey put his hand on her arm "Wait up" he told her, he took the AK 47 that had been the guard's and held it in front of her "Know about one of these?" he asked her.

"Of course I bloody well do" Sandy was indignant, "I've done the training"

"I'm not talking about the stuff you see in training, they use the ones on sale in the USA" He replied, "this is an original, it's got a few extras not seen in the west" He carried on. "Here on the safety, you've got four settings not the two sold in the US" Joey pointed to the little handle above the trigger, "Safe, single shot just like the ones we see in the west, then you've got 'double tap' as in two shots and fully automatic fire" he handed the weapon to her, "here, you'll need the extra firepower when things really kick off!"

She took the rifle, checking the safety; it was on 'safe' with the magazine attached. "How fast can it shoot?"

"We're clear" Jacko's voice broke in over the radio. Joey signalled her to follow him "Roger, we're on our way" he carried on to Sandy, "that Magazine holds thirty rounds; on fully automatic it'll empty the magazine in just under three seconds"

"That's six hundred rounds a minute!" Sandy was a bit shocked, "Same as a heavy machine gun!"

They were at the door of the Command post as Joey replied "Yep, and its handheld!" they stepped into the room.

The room was pretty spartan with three tables around the walls of the building, in the northwest corner was a trap door that opened up on a set of stairs leading down to the lower levels, in the northeast corner was another set of steps leading to another door that lead onto the roof where the antennae were. The tables were on the western, southern and eastern walls with a cabinet housing the computer servers on the northern wall. The cabinet was only waist height with a large monitor above it, there were four screens on the monitor, one of them, the top right one showed Chambers in a cell with the light on.

The evidence of a quick, efficient and ruthless entry was there, three operators were in the corner, dragged there by Jacko and Mac, their weapons all removed and piled in the middle, their jackets removed, one of them had his boots, socks and trousers removed, they all had small a small hole that went through the roof of the mouth and exited at the base of the skull at the back of the head, evidence of a silenced 9mm in the hands of experts, they had no chance to give a warning.

"Gather the Intel and set the charges" Jacko was all business, they'd scooped up one of the AK 47s and two or three magazines, even Chambers was going to have to help with firepower! "We're going for Chambers" he signalled to Mac they were both wearing the jackets they'd 'acquired'. "How long do you need?"

"Seven minutes boss" Joey replied, "Then all hell breaks loose, don't forget I need the Oxygen cylinders!" he was already unpacking some little packages he'd brought along, "Sandy. We can use these bags for any laptops, do you need the hard drives from those servers?" he pointed to the cabinet.

Sandy had already done a quick scan of the room, she had to remind herself these men they'd killed were working for people who happily brought murder, death and destruction onto the streets in nearly every city in Europe, and all for the almighty dollar, they got everything they deserved and compared to the deaths they inflicted Jacko and Mac had been very merciful! "Yeah," she replied, "Let's grab as much as we can"

Joey smashed the cabinet with the butt of one of the AK 47s. It took him another fifteen seconds to smash the back off the computers and rip the hard drives out, no need to worry about leaving evidence, the 'little packages' would take care of that.

Those little packages were a half a pound of C4 with a small timing detonator that he set to seven minutes, when they went up they'd take most of this side of the fortress with them. He placed three of them in a corner of the room, then he took the oxygen cylinders, they were still quarter full, that was great. It was all he needed. He opened the valve slightly on the cylinders and placed them upright with the valve on the top inside the computers servers. The idea was simple; the C4 would go up and heat the room to around five hundred degrees Celsius, which would ignite the oxygen in the cavity, the flame would travel down inside the valve like a rocket driving the cylinder itself down and through the wooden floorboards causing them to ignite and set the floor below ablaze, hopefully if the armoury was below as they suspected that would cause the munitions to start 'cooking off' as well as the CP causing absolute havoc and panic!

Joey had two more C4 packages to plant and set, each one had slightly less time on the timer so that they could go off all at the same time as the others, he signalled they needed to go onto the roof, "Just in case they've got another phone line somewhere" he'd explained, "I want to make sure the antennae are as dead as dodos!" Sandy grabbed one of the handhelds that the CP people had.

Joey'd just planted the last of the explosive and was heading for the steps back down when the radio came to life, it was in Russian so he didn't understand it, but he did understand Sandy's cussing!

"What?"

"Guard commander can't find one of his men," she said, "So he's trying the CP and worried why they're not replying, he's coming!"

"Oh shit" he flicked his mike on, "Boss, we got company!"

"Roger, how much a problem?"

"Guard commander inbound to the CP maybe ten seconds"

"Any chance of exit?"

"Negative, we're on the roof, not seen yet, but only one minute on the timers"

"Roger," Jacko did not sound happy. "Go for the base"

'Base' was a code they'd agreed on for the last resort in the escape, it was bloody dangerous even in daylight, at night it was damn near suicidal, but there was no choice, they were going to have to base jump and use the wingsuits to glide off the building!

"I always knew you were bloody crazy" Sandy muttered to Joey as he helped her rig the wingsuit, it took about ten seconds to unzip the sleeves, unfold the material and zip back up to the main body, the same with the legs, "I look like a frog!!" the humour was helping with releasing tension.

"Just as long as there are no plans for croaking" Joey replied with a smile. Sandy wanted to throw something at him the humour was so bad!

The noise downstairs was starting as the guard commander tried the door, it was jammed as they'd wedged a table up against it, and he began shouting into the radio. Shots were fired into the door.

As soon as they were ready Joey waddled over to the edge, "You ready?"He asked.

The guard commander was calling up the other guards in the guard hut near the front of the fortress, they began to pour out of the hut in a state of semi preparedness, and weapons at the ready were brought to bear on the figures they could see on the roof. The shit was about to fly, and so were they.

"You are kidding?" Sandy shot back, she was terrified, but even a near-suicidal 'base jump' was better than what awaited them if they hung around; at least there was a small chance of living through it!

"Remember" Joey shouted as he jumped, "Spread your legs and make a star formation, now follow me" and with that, he jumped. The wind caught him and he was away.

"Lunatic" Sandy screamed more at Joey than at herself as she followed suit less than a tenth of a second after him, the wind caught them and they were away speeding as the world erupted behind them.

Chapter 10

"Gather the Intel and set the charges" Jacko was all business, they'd scooped up one of the AK 47s and two or three magazines, even Chambers was going to have to help with firepower! "We're going for Chambers" he signalled to Mac they were both wearing the jackets they'd 'acquired'. "How long do you need?"

"Seven minutes boss" Joey replied, "Then all hell breaks loose, and don't forget I need those Oxygen cylinders!" he said pointing to the cylinders they were still wearing, he was already unpacking some little packages he'd brought along, "Sandy. We can use these bags for any laptops, do you need the hard drives from those servers?" he pointed to the cabinet.

Jacko and Mac didn't hear the reply as they were heading down the steps to the lower levels. The first of the 'lower' levels was the accommodation block for the CP staff, they could hear a couple of people snoring so they moved on down quickly and quietly, about halfway down

Jacko who as the team leader was also the team linguist started speaking in Russian.

"We need to transfer the prisoner to Tehran" he was explaining to Mac who had no idea what was being said but knew it was a ruse so he went along with it.

"Da" was all Mac said in reply

At the bottom of the stairs was a metal door, the bars were across on the other side, it was locked, Mac stepped up and banged hard on the door, "Offen das tur" he shouted in German.

They had no idea what languages the men behind the door spoke, but being either Spetznaz or foreign legion there was a good chance they all understood German so they were playing the idea of legionaries sent to transport Chambers to another place.

"On whose orders?" the reply came back, "Who told you to transfer?"

"Don't bloody argue" Jacko shot back, the exchange had changed to Russian "The bosses want him out of here; you want to argue with them?"

"I want to see the paperwork first" the reply came back; someone was looking through the spyglass in the door. They held up a piece of paper to the glass, it was filled with Cyrillic script but neither of them had an idea what it was, and it was too far away for the man to read. "Hold it closer" the word came back.

"Just open the flaming door you stupid prick!" Jacko shot back "Or I'll have your balls for breakfast!"

They heard the bolt slide back and the door began to open. As it swung both stepped through raised their pistols and fired. Even silenced weapons make a sound, granted not as loud as normal ones, but the sound isn't totally eliminated, just muted. Jacko had taken out the man opening the door before it even had time to register what was happening, Mac stepped through and took out his mate who almost got his hand on his Makarov.

There were four doors leading off from the room, Chambers' room had the light on, but they also had the light on in the guard's station so they couldn't really tell which room he was in.

There was no need to give dumb orders, he and Mac began searching, they found Chambers in the third room. He was semi-awake with bloodshot eyes and looked as if he hadn't washed in days, classic sleep deprivation technique.

One of the most efficient way of 'softening a target up' before interrogation is simply depriving them of sleep, food and water. Give them no food or water and simply keep the light on, when they eventually settle down to try and sleep turn on the stereo and blast them with heavy rock music, or any kind of noise, then when you've got them fully awake turn the noise off and begin again, when they are almost asleep do the same again. The beauty of the system is that there's no real effort required on your part!

Keep that up and after two or three days their head is so sore from either dehydration or lack of sleep they're ready to give you what you want, hell people have even confessed to murders they weren't anywhere near after two or three days in Police custody before now. Naturally being MI6 Chambers was trained to withstand that torture, but that would only have been the beginning as it sets him up perfectly for what was planned next.

Jacko stepped into the cell "Steve" he spoke softly as he approached the figure huddled in the corner, "It's me, Jacko; we're here to take you home buddy"

"Took you bloody long enough" Chambers broke out into a huge smile as he gave his mate a weak hug, "Rest of the team here too?"

'Chambers may look like crap' Jacko thought as they got him to his feet, 'but he's all here mentally' they headed for the cell door, "Mac's here with some good stuff! He pointed to Mac who as the medic was preparing some sort of drink for him, "Joey and Smithy are doing their things, we've got about two minutes before Joey makes his presence felt"

"That short" Steve knew Joey of old, he was the one recruited him from the Engineers back a couple of years ago, one of the best bomb disposal experts he'd ever come across, consequently not someone you want building a booby trap you get caught by!

"Here, take this and stop talking while I give you a quick examination" Mac handed Steve the drink; it tasted foul, just like seawater with sugar in! Which is pretty much what an Oral rehydration pack is, but with a few vitamins and minerals added.

Foul or not Chambers downed it in one, "You're meant to sip the bloody thing" Mac muttered in his ear, just then the radio came alive in their ears.

"Boss, we got company!"

"Roger, how much a problem?"

"Guard commander inbound to the CP maybe ten seconds"

"Any chance of an exit?"

"Negative, we're on the roof, not seen yet, but only one minute on the timers"

"Roger, go for the Base"

Jacko turned to Chambers and handed him the clothing that was on the desk, "Quick, change and put these on, give us your old stuff here and hurry up"

Steve handed the old clothes to Jacko who'd undressed one of the guards, he quickly put the clothes onto the corpse of one of the guards and they threw the body into the cell, with luck the explosion would level the building and the cave in would leave them with an unrecognizable body here, giving them idea that Chambers was killed in the blast, that was the plan at least.

The plan was so simple it was almost ludicrous, actually, that's what Sandy said it was when she first heard it, they were simply going to walk out and jump in a Landcruiser while Joey blows up the building. The plan had been that Joey and Sandy were going to be with them, that changed with the guard commander showing up, but the rest of the plan was still a 'go'.

They got to ground level as the first shots rang out; the rest of the guards had seen Joey and Sandy on the roof and were shouting orders as well as trying to shoot.

"Smithy" Jacko spoke softly, "any help you can give Joey?"

"They're all good boss, I've got the guards panicking, there were a couple of oil drums they forgot about, they're on fire now though, you're clear for the exit"

"Roger that" he clicked the mike off and turned to the other two, "You folks ready?"

"Born ready boss" Mac replied with a smile, "And he'll come even if I have to drag his arse out of here"

"You'll get no complaints from me" Steve replied. "Don't recommend this hotel anyway!" that drew a smile.

"Then let's go" they literally got up and walked into the courtyard as if they owned the place and headed for the first Landcruiser, Jacko climbed into the driver's seat with Chambers next to him, Mac took up the back seat, as soon as he was in he unstrapped the Commando and set the switch to 'grenade launcher'

They were almost at the gate when a huge bang erupted into the night, it was as if the whole of the night behind them abandoned the darkness and took on the form of a great fireball as two and a half kilograms of C4 blew the building apart, men were thrown ten to fifteen feet back, drums were flying through the air and chaos was evident.

"No one leaves the compound" a voice shouted, "Stop that vehicle" attention was drawn their way, the gates began to close.

"Smithy" Jacko screamed into the mike, "Take the towers out NOW!!"

Within a couple of seconds, two men fell, one out of each tower, blown out by the force of the round that had taken half their heads off, smithy's voice came over the mike "That fast enough boss?"

They were in third gear doing about thirty miles an hour when they hit the half closed splintering the gates and almost knocking the guards down, shots were ringing around them, one took out the wing mirror, another passed through the windscreen between the driver and passenger, they heard a yelp from Mac. Shit, that meant he was hit,

"Don't worry boss, just a scratch" he quickly reassured them, a little too quickly, but they couldn't do much about it.

The 'scratch' was actually a 'through and through' in his arm, there were no bones broken and as far as he could tell he could still use the arm, the blood loss was small, but no time to stop and bandage it, the other Landcruisers were starting up. Mac punched out the rear glass and readied the grenade launcher, "Boss, give me five seconds at the first turn with no movement!"

"Will do Mac, make it count" they'd almost have to crawl around the hairpin anyway, he braked hard, "Hang on" he came to a sudden stop.

The first of the other Landcruisers was just passing the mangled gates when it was hit with a massive ball of fire travelling at about eight hundred miles an hour in the opposite direction, the grenade made short work of the vehicle stopping it dead in its tracks and flipping it end over end, the vehicle ended up on its roof, the entrance was blocked and the building on fire, that momentary stop allowed them to see firsthand the result of the night's work.

The gates were ablaze with men running around frantically trying to put out the fires there, but further back where the keep had been was just a mass of rocks engulfed in a fire that lit up the whole sky, it was as if someone had lit a huge beacon fire like in Lord of the Rings calling Gondor's allies to war, and like Gondor Phoenix would use her allies to hunt them down.

"Let's get a move on" Jacko was the first to break the silence, "Smithy's at the second turn down and we've only got a few hours to get you over the border before all hell breaks loose diplomatically"

"What about Joey?" Steve shouted over the noise," and who's with him?"

"Joey's got a new spook with him" Mac replied, he'd taken the moment to put a field dressing on, the wound was good and although it hurt like hell there was no way he was letting the boss know that "You know her, Sandy Little" he was gingerly putting his jacket back on as Jacko put the vehicle into gear, "They're making a run for the border, place called 'Penjuin' I think, at least that was the backup plan!"

"But that's nearly two hundred flaming miles" Steve was shocked. Surely we can do something to help?"

"Joey won't need our help but God help Iran if the Iranians get in his way" Jacko replied, "He'll blow everything up knowing him! The best thing we can do is to get you to the border then look for the trail of destruction and see where it's heading, you can guarantee he'll be at the head of it!"

Sandy was terrified, the Halo had been terrifying yet fun, this was just sheer terror, the ground was whistling by below them less than a hundred feet away, yet they were picking up speed and didn't seem to be getting any closer to the ground, then all of a sudden it disappeared, only to reappear directly ahead of them as she heard Joey shout "Left hand and foot down now" she did so and found herself performing a steep banking motion as they skirted the edge of the cliff, she swore if she'd tried she could have touched the mountain.

Just ahead of them she could see something or maybe things running, it was only a few seconds later that she realized it was a flock of sheep, the shepherds had heard the explosion and came to look only to see two black-clad things that looked like bats coming down on them at incredible speed, convinced they were being attacked by evil spirits or 'Jinn' as they are known in the Islamic world they were half running and half turning and firing their AK47s at the apparitions in a 'spray and pray routine' as they fled screaming "Allah U Akbar" trying to ward off these evil demons!

"You OK?" Joey asked through the mike he was slightly ahead.

"I'm hurtling through the night at some ridiculous speed, no idea where we're going, being shot at by locals who think I'm a demon with a maniac adrenaline junkie and you ask if I'm OK?"

"Well. Are you?"

"No bullet holes if that counts"

"Good" Joey didn't even seem to notice the insults she'd just hurled at him, "Get ready for landing" ten seconds later he gave the word "Pull" and they both reached for their ripcords again, the chutes opened and a few seconds later they were on the ground.

Chapter 11

Alexander Gregorovitch was furious, not just your average everyday type of furious, but an absolute blood vessel bursting needing to strangle the first one who crosses him type furious! Somehow somebody had sent a team of Special Forces into the fortress that he was in charge of and wreaked absolute havoc.

Whoever it was had somehow gotten two hundred miles into Iran, past all their allies, into the Lion's den totally undetected and wreaked incredible devastation, how the hell was he going to answer for this? 'Who the hell were they?' was his immediate thought, there'd be time to sit and work that out later, but for now, he needed to find out just how much damage was done, and track these swine down, hunt them down like the dogs they were!

The fires were under control, the Command building was totally gutted, two levels were just heaps of burned stone and rubble, the third level, the dungeons had collapsed ceilings, the last floor had the walls still intact, but the rubble from the other floors were in the cells.

The front of the fortress was a little better, at least only the gates there were burned, there were only the gates capable of burning there, the burned-out hulk of what used to be a Toyota Landcruiser flipped onto its roof and facing the wrong way, the smell of cooked flesh was strong there.

"Get that heap out the way" he screamed at the men trying to shift the vehicle, they were rocking the vehicle trying to get it back onto its wheels, or wheel rims so they could use one of the other Toyotas to shunt it out of the gates where they can push it off the road. "And where's that chopper?" he took a Satellite phone out of his pocket punched in a number and carried on his rant "Get your idle arse into your chopper and get everyone and I mean everyone here NOW! I want search teams on the ground and searching within the hour DO YOU UNDERSTAND?"

Whoever he screamed at clearly did understand as he heard the turbines starting as he hung up, turned to the nearest man and shouted "I want all commanders we have left in my accommodation in ten minutes with damage reports and casualty estimates, pass the word" turned and stormed off, now to get the Iranians involved.

General Omar Sherhaz was only dozing when the phone rang, he lifted the receiver on the second ring, "What?" he shouted angrily into the handset, more frustrated at not being able to sleep than disturbed at the phone ringing at this ungodly hour.

"Sorry to wake you General" It was Gregorovitch on the line, "but we have a situation with the pipeline, we've had a terrorist attack on the pipeline"

"WHAT?" the General bolted out of bed, "When? Where?" he made a grab for his clothing, his aide came running in with a message that had just come off the fax machine, there'd been an attempt to blow up the Gas pipeline, the report said it was unsuccessful but a second attack at the security company's HQ at Alamut had caused some damage! He stood waiting for the General to indicate he wanted the report. "How bad?" he asked down the line.

"The Pipeline itself isn't damaged, but Alamut has sustained moderate damage" Gregorovitch continued, "My men killed some" he lied, "but we've got at least five or so still at large and fleeing westwards!"

"Those Damned Iraqi sons of dogs" The General screamed, "I presume that in calling me you want my men involved in a manhunt?" he asked.

"The sooner we catch these terrorists the better" Gregorovitch led the conversation, he wanted the General to buy into the idea of taking credit for mounting the manhunt, that way he'd get more co-operation.

"I'll mobilize the Republican Guard" The General spoke a command to both his aide and the phone line, "You'll have roadblocks and search parties within the hour throughout the whole northwest, a hundred-mile radius, will that be enough?"

"That will be wonderful General" Gregorovitch commented, "But there is one more request I have"

"Don't bother me with little things Gregorovitch" the General shouted into the phone, "Just do what you need to in finding these people, you have control, but you will answer to me, GOT THAT! Now, bring in what you need!" with that, he slammed the phone down and shouted "Anis, get my car ready, it appears there's a lot of work to do this morning"

Joey and Sandy came to a stop in a field, by some miracle neither of them had been hit and apart from Sandy still shaking.

"Hey, it's alright" he said softly as he placed a hand on each shoulder, gently pulling her to himself in a brotherly hug, "We're out, we're safe" he held her for a moment before looking directly into her face "It's OK to admit you're afraid you know"

"Huh" that wasn't what she expected to hear from this 'tough guy', "I'm alright, I think I'm alright really" she didn't sound all that convinced"

"I didn't think anything else" Joey replied, "but I do want you to know that it's okay to admit to being afraid! It's not being afraid that's the problem, or even admitting it, that's healthy, it' what you do with that fear that counts!" he turned and started gathering the parachutes up.

"What are you on about" Sandy was s bit stumped, it's not what she expected to hear, she'd been trying so hard to hide her fear, so desperately wanting to appear to be one of them, she started gathering the 'chutes' "are we repacking these?" she tried changing the subject.

"No. Not really" he explained, "It's going to be light in a couple of hours, they'll be after us then and the villages will give them a good idea of the way we went, it's only going to take them about an hour or so to find where we landed, then everyone and his dog will be after us!"

"This is Iran" she replied, "They hate dogs here!"

"This is KURDISH Iran" he replied, "The Kurds use dogs for guarding their sheep, I'm surprised we didn't run into a couple last night, and I'm really thankful we didn't as they're about the meanest things in these mountains, bred for hunting and killing!" he pointed to some bushes about a hundred meters away that they could just make out in the moonlight "We'll hide the 'chutes' in there, they'll find them pretty quick, but there's a road a couple of miles away, hopefully, they'll put two and two together to come up with five and think we're meeting up on the road there"

"But Jacko and the rest headed northwest" She replied, "we're south!"

"There's a road that joins their road a couple of miles from the fortress, but you're right, they're heading northwest and will try and loop round but further out, they'll work out that our RV point is about fifteen miles away, west of here and we've got four hours" he peeled back his suit to look at his watch, "Hopefully this will buy us a couple of hours while they look the wrong way!"

'But we're heading for that place, what's it called? Penjuin?" Sandy was confused. "Aren't we?"

"That's the last resort plan" Joey explained, "we always have a 'last resort' like that, and this seems the best time to start thinking about the last resort with the way things are going"

"Did you even consider going for the original 'backup'?" Sandy asked.

"Not really" Joey replied truthfully, "It's too near the fortress, Jacko put it in the plan as a way to confuse the enemy, let them think you're heading for that while at the same time heading for your true destination. Jacko and the team will pass it and check it out, but any problems and they'll let us know so we can keep going." He was very 'matter of fact' in the way he delivered it, she wondered if she really understood the way they thought.

It took them ten minutes to 'hide the chutes' enough time that made it look like a hasty but plausible location and not something that might be a trick, then they were ready to move, Joey'd already explained the way they were going to go, literally taking the most direct route, over any obstacle in the way, that was a high ridge between two peaks. Joey was in the lead, but Sandy was only a couple of paces behind.

"What did you mean about 'what you do with your fear'?" she asked as they made their way up the mountain.

"Being afraid is natural" he replied, 'and good, it'll keep you sharp in a dangerous situation, but if you let that fear paralyse you then it's going to kill you!"

"Yeah, I know that" Sandy replied, "the old fight or flight response"

"Yep, both of those are valid responses" Joey went on, "But the being 'afraid' can be used to help you make sure you prepare properly for the 'fight' when you realise you're afraid then you pay more attention to what your senses tell you, that'll keep you alive as the brain takes notice more of what's happening around, you make sure your equipment is working properly, and then the 'fear' makes sure you check it again, just to make sure it is! That's what I mean by what you do with the fear"

"Is that why you're constantly checking the equipment?" she asked, trying not to sound offensive.

"Partly" Joey replied, "using the natural instinct to give me the edge the good Lord meant me to have, making sure I do my best to come through the fight in one piece, and bring my mates through it as well!" he held up his hand, he'd heard something, very faint but there it was again, Sandy heard it too this time. They both froze, and then very slowly went to ground behind some rocks.

It was still semi-dark so they had the advantage but if they could hear then they could be heard, it was a human voice they'd heard and it was coming closer, the safeties were flicked to 'double shot' hopefully they wouldn't be seen but better to be ready, Mr Colt and Mr Kalashnikov were ready 'to speak' if need be.

"Joey and Sandy got away clean boss" Smithy spoke as he climbed into the spare seat in the Landcruiser; he'd been at the meeting point waiting as they came down the mountain. They were on the move again.

"At least that's good news" Jacko replied relieved, though they hated that the team had gotten split up "What direction?"

"They were heading South, down the valley that way!" the 'Cruiser' was picking up speed, "I'd say he's going be at the RV in a couple of hours!"

There was no 'pursuit' from the fortress, but anything could be happening, they were keeping an eye on the road for any signs of problems coming from there, so far there was none.

Everything went well for about fifteen minutes, they were making good time and would be at there with an hour or so to spare, then disaster struck, they were slowing down.

"What's wrong?" it was Chambers who asked what the other two were thinking.

"Engine's overheating" Jacko replied, "We'd better have a look before she packs up altogether!"

They pulled off the road onto a dirt track and hid the vehicle in some bushes, "Mac, you take a look at the engine" Jacko spoke turning to Mac, "Smithy and I'll take up defensive positions until you tell us what's needed"

"Okay boss" Mac replied, "Steve, you stay with me OK?" he got out, Jacko popped the hood and got out, he and Smithy took up defensive positions, one at the front and one at the back.

It took Mac about a minute to find the problem, "Boss, we got a bullet wedged in the radiator, but I think I saw what we need just a little way back, we'll be back in about ten minutes." He turned to Steve, "Come on, I'll need your help, Grab those spare water canteens"

Ten minutes later they were back with water bottles filled and a couple of eggs, "Shit Mac!" Smithy exclaimed, "We're in deep shit and you're thinking about bloody breakfast?"

"Sorry Smithy" Mac replied with a grin, "I know you love my gourmet meals, but this is to fix the radiator with!" and with that, he took a canteen mug from off the top of his water bottle, cracked the eggs and poured the whites of the eggs into the mug. Next, he took the top off the radiator and poured the egg white into the radiator.

Taking a roll of duct tape he wrapped the end round the hose that had been creased by the bullet, he kept wrapping it round until the hope was tightly sealed and firm, then he cut the roll. "fire her up boss" he told Jacko.

Jacko did and as soon as the engine started Mac poured the water into the radiator until the radiator was full, then he put the cap back on and closed the hood, "Right boys" he turned to the two still stood there, "That should hold for about thirty miles or so, but the radiator is completely buggered after that, let's get the hell out of here"

"Boss, get this shit off the road NOW" Mac screamed as they came round the corner, he was watching their backs and had just caught a glimpse of their worst nightmare, Jacko floored the gas and found the first place he could get off the road then floored it as he headed for cover, anything would do. They just made it when a BMP 2 troop carrier came round the bend loaded with troops and guns bristling, it was the lead vehicle in the lead element of a massive convoy. The Iranians were looking for them and they were bringing serious firepower!

Chapter 12

22,000 miles above the site something was watching, catching every little detail and relaying the information back down to the earth some seven to ten thousand miles away, across continents and oceans where the information was about to cause absolute panic.

For years the West has had a major distrust of Iran and all things Iranian, ever since the regime came to power in the late 1970s there seemed to be no middle ground on which both Iran and the west could agree, it didn't help that the biggest power in the west was literally caught with its 'pants down' when the revolution happened and not only backed the wrong players but was caught 'red handed' spying on the new regime, something that caused a major standoff that lasted over a year and caused major embarrassment to all concerned.

Langley went ballistic! Major explosions in Iran so close to a major pipeline, and then talk on the intercepted calls of 'terrorism' and 'terrorists' threw them for a loop. In Langley's language, the two words Iran and terrorism were almost never on opposite sides of the ledger! They were virtually synonymous with each other.

Phone lines were going crazy as more and more analysts were calling in to ask "What the hell?" or basically "How the hell did someone do this without us knowing about it? And who the hell is responsible?" No one was looking forward to telling the President!

Tel Aviv was even worse, things like this have a tendency to get blamed on 'The son of Shaytan' as the Iranians loved to call Israel so they'd be expecting to at least to know what they're going to get blamed for, and having an irate Prime Minister on the phone wanting to know what the hell they were being accused of was not a pleasant experience, dealing with President Obama when he wasn't happy was bad enough, Benjamin Netanyahu was positively dangerous, he'd been known to throw things and not just in general but at you, and they tended to hit their target!

Downing Street called an immediate meeting of 'C.O.B.R.A' the emergency response team of the security services, everyone was scared this could escalate into something bigger, the Iranians and Israelis both have nuclear arsenals and even the slightest hint that Israel was involved could set the 'hounds of hell' loose and the way the Iranians were mobilizing it seemed that's what was happening!

One thing that was on everyone's mind but no one wanted to say it was could Isis be behind the attack? Isis are Sunni Muslims but the Iranians are Shiite, a divide that's filled with fourteen centuries of hatred and bloodshed! Could they be resurrecting the centuries-old blood feud in some crazy way?

There was one place that was watching the events unfold yet was a sea of relative peace, that was Sir Michael's office, not MI6 (that was in uproar) but his inner sanctum, with the doors closed and jamming devices blocking any signal trying to intercept what was going on in the office. He would still be able to call out though. He was watching the satellite feed that MI6 had hacked from one of the US spy satellites over Iran.

MI6 had an official link to the satellite but he knew that it was heavily censored by Langley so that it showed them only what Langley wanted them to see, so they hacked a couple of other ways in so they could get a better picture without letting on they had the other information, Langley knew they'd done it but it met with the idea that kept the politicians happy that no one was 'giving away' secrets. Langley had done the same with the British networks, everyone knew and yet no one knew!

"Brenda" Sir Michael pressed the button on his intercom, "I'll expect the PM to call any minute, can you tell him to come right over please?"

"Sir" the receptionist replied, "He's already on the line demanding you go over there right now!"

"Sorry Brenda" Sir Michael replied, "No can do right at this moment, tell him I have his answers, but for his ears only and they're not leaving this room! Tell him I'll be free in about fifteen minutes" he clicked the intercom off and unplugged it, 'Probably get the sack' he thought, 'but this is too important and too delicate to be let known everywhere'. Reaching into his pocket he pulled out a mobile and punched in a number.

The number was pre-set on the speed dial and rang on the other side of the continent.

The recipient answered on the second ring, "Glad to see you're awake down there" Sir Michael spoke into the phone, "We're on scrambler aren't we?"

"I am" the reply came back, "I presume your end is secure too" it was the Colonel.

"Just a quick update, they got in" Sir Michael spoke softly as if that would make a difference.

"So that's what the panic is about" Simpson replied. "You should see the headless chickens running about here!" you could hear the amusement in the voice, "I take it from what's happening things aren't as easy as we'd hoped?"

"They never are, but it looks as if young Metcalfe is doing his hardest to create enough havoc for the rest of the team to get away, from what I can make out they may have had to split up to make their escape"

"Jacko said something about that just before the drop" Simpson spoke up filling in some of the blanks in the plan, "They weren't sure at the time, but young Metcalfe worked in the region before joining the regiment, he knows the ways out there"

"He was in Iraq though, not Iran right?" Sir Michael was a little confused

"Officially yes" Simpson replied, "But I know he took at least one unofficial trip over to the border, if not over it with some Kurdish folks. What direction are they heading?"

"One group went out by the road, heading southwest, the other, looks like they headed south and I'm not sure I want to know how they got out!"

"You're right there" the colonel chuckled, "guy's a bit of an adrenaline junkie even for a 'blade' but I've got a pretty good idea where they're headed, we've got our side all ready to go, I'm moving us to Erbil in about ten minutes, there's an Iraqi airbase there that the commander's agreed to let us work from" he stopped for a moment then continued, "any calls and we can be there in ten minutes"

"Good to hear, now I've got to go, I've an irate prime minister to 'educate'" Sir Michael clicked the phone off, closed it up and put it into his desk drawer, just then Brenda buzzed to tell him that the prime minister had arrived along with the minister of defence, he told her to show the pm in but under no circumstances was the minister of defence to be allowed in, apart from himself and David Cameron everyone else was under suspicion until the mole was found, and if that made him enemies well he could live with that.

"Just what the hell are you doing telling me who and whom I can't bring to a meeting with my own head of intelligence?" David Cameron stormed into the room in a fury, he didn't even bother with the pleasantries or wait to be 'announced' as protocol would normally dictate.

"Good morning to you too Prime minister" Sir Michael tried to diffuse the situation, "If you'll take a seat I'll explain some of what I can" he indicated to the prime minister to take a seat. Cameron was refusing to.

"I've got the bloody Americans screaming all kinds of stuff, the Israelis ready to launch a nuke strike 'as a precaution' and we haven't got a bloody clue, then when I try and call you I get some cryptic BS about having some of the answers, what the hell are you up to?"

Sir Michael hadn't risen from his chair, he'd hardly taken his eyes off the computer screen, but now he took a moment to make eye contact. "I said I could tell you some of it, enough get you to persuade the Israelis and Americans that we don't need a 'strike' and I will, but you need to shut up and listen!" he was getting pretty frustrated.

The prime minister finally calmed down enough to sit down and say "Okay, you've got two minutes before I fire you! Go ahead"

"Remember the bombs in Istanbul?" Sir Michael began.

"What the hell has a terrorist threat got to do with this?"

"They weren't terrorists" Sir Michael countered, "we were meant to think they were." He stopped for a moment to let that sink in. Then, pressing a button on his desk a large flat screen TV came to life, he'd already set the details of what he wanted up so he went straight into it. "They were a cover for them to kidnap this diplomat"Chambers' face came onto the screen.

"The Iranians going to all that trouble for a bloody diplomat? Give me a break" he was rising from his chair.

"Who said the Iranians?" Sir Michael shot back; "in this game, you need to know who the real enemy is" Cameron stopped dead and began paying attention.

"The diplomat has the kind of intelligence that in the wrong hands will blow every operation both we and the Americans have run against certain 'criminal gangs' as well as Islamic terrorists for the last five years! And that's just a conservative estimate" he paused for a moment then continued, "I'm talking hundreds, if not thousands of lives at stake and billions of dollars, we couldn't let that happen, not at any price"

Cameron was silent for a moment as he took it in, "but if it's just a lone operative then why not a drone strike? It's easy and clean"

Sir Michael actually wanted to throttle the man for even suggesting that, but then again the PM was thinking of the political fallout from the idea of a team getting caught in Iran and being traced back to Britain as opposed to a 'drone strike' that went 'off target' by a mere two hundred miles! He took his time responding. "Mr PM, there's a reason I said for your ears only" he began, "There were only three people in the world knew the Intelligence that diplomat had, one's here in the room with you, another is the diplomat and the third is the young MI6 operative with the team of ex SAS soldiers trying to break him out, how the hell the enemy got the intelligence we don't know as yet, but one thing we do know is we have a problem! Mr PM, we have a serious breach in our security and the only way to find that leak is to bust that man out, that's what they're doing!"

"And destroying any kind of agreement we've had with Iran in the process!" Cameron shot back, "are you folks totally off your trolleys with this?" he demanded, "the political ramifications are" he began.

"Will never get out" Sir Michael cut him off, "The Iranians are about to realize they've been played for the patsies! They employed the same security firm that's in cahoots with the drug barons and they were using the fortress in Iran as their safe house thinking we'd never attempt to take them on in the 'devils playground' they got that wrong."

"How many people know about this?"

"About the breakout?" Sir Michael asked. "Only eight in total and six of them are on the ground in Iran, Colonel Simpson is in Iraq with a couple of Longbows and a spare Lynx, then there's you and me, that's it"

"What about the Americans and Iraqis?"

"As I said, Mr PM, there's a leak, and until we know where it is no one can know, not even the Defence Minister!"

Chapter 13

Joey and Sandy waited unable to move in case the villagers saw them, so far they hadn't and they had no idea just how close to a sudden and unexpected meeting with their maker they came to as they moved on under the steady track of the Colt and the Kalashnikov in Joey and Sandy's hands.

"That puts paid to going that way" Joey was looking around for an alternative to where they were headed, the villagers had walked down the path they were intending to take, and it was clear they were looking for something or someone, both the villagers had been carrying AK47s which was pretty much a part of standard dress code in the villages round here this was Kurdistan region and Kurdistan is a law unto itself!

There was a wooded area west south-west of where they were, it seemed to disappear over the hill and possibly joined the forest that was on the other side of the valley, there was a risk it didn't and they'd be left exposed but they couldn't carry on the path they were on as the villagers would be back, and there just might be more of them.

"How long do you think it's going to add to the journey?" Sandy asked as she began to follow Joey, she'd learned to trust him in these decisions.

"Not sure" he replied, "I just know we can't keep on the same path, there's usually a path in the woods we can follow, one the smugglers use to move from village to village without the authorities knowing about them"

"And you know this because?" she was really curious as there's been nothing in any of the briefings to show how he knew this!

"You read my file?" It was more a statement saying 'You should know' but he continued, "A couple of years ago I worked training some of the Kurdish militia in Iraq, training in Bomb disposal" he moved through the wood, "Most of the guys I was training had spent time in Iran, some worked as smugglers, bootleggers believe it or not!"

"Bootleggers? This is Iran you know?" she stopped and looked at Joey's back, 'really, at times some of the most ridiculous things come out of that boy's mouth! "It's not 1930s Kentucky"

"What? You surprised that the Mullahs like their booze?" Joey turned laughing slightly, "It might be banned by Islam" he continued "But they're just as human as the rest of us, and they love their Johnny Walker red label!"

"You're a mine of information like this" Sandy half-joked back, she was tired and while the verbal duelling had been amusing, and even helped to take her mind off the more pressing fears she couldn't help liking having her own 'walking encyclopaedia' walking through this wood with her.

The movies always show military convoys as seemingly endless lines of trucks and a tank rolling down a road, the reality is something different. The vehicles are usually grouped in blocks of four to six called 'packets' where each vehicle within the 'packet' stay within sight of each other, but there might be as much as two or three miles between each 'packet'.

The first packet took only about two minutes to roll past, but it was the two most intense and nerve-racking minutes they'd had since the mission started, all it would take was for the commander in the BMP to rotate the turret and they were screwed!

"Go, Get the hell out of here" Mac whispered as soon as the last vehicle in that first packet disappeared round the bend, they possibly had seconds before the next would appear. Jacko dropped the vehicle into gear and they drove off down the dirt path they'd turned onto.

About two miles further in they came to a crossroads, each track led to a village, there was no real way they could safely get back onto the road in this Landcruiser, there was only one thing for it, they had to chance passing through one of the villages, and that meant they'd need a vehicle when they got to the other side!

The Iranians were setting up roadblocks on the main road, that meant they knew some of the team had gotten out using a vehicle, they probably had the details of the vehicle that was used and it was only a matter of time before they had the resources to start going into the villages and searching from village to village, what was worse was that the villagers themselves would take part in the searching.

The only chance they had was to put as much ground between them and the searchers as they possibly could and to send their pursuers a clear message, "If you want to live then BACK OFF!!"

Gregorovitch was looking pleased with himself, finally, things were starting to come together. The fires in the compound were finally under control, the mess that was a Landcruiser and the gates were removed and re-enforcements were beginning to arrive.

The makeshift Command post was down in the village at the foot of the mountain as they began to organize the search for the people responsible, he was looking at the map he'd pinned on the far wall of the building and thinking. 'Okay, if I was you, what would be my move?' when one of his commanders burst into the room.

"Sir" he began, "one of the villagers has located where the parachutists landed" he moved forward and looked at the map; "If I may" he lifted a pointer and pointed to the valley to the south of the fortress. "Here sir, about five miles south of the fortress, we found the parachutes just off the main valley and about half a mile from the road here" he indicated the thin red line running east to west, "the road takes them right to the border"

"You're thinking that they RV'd with the Landcruiser there?" Gregorovitch asked, "And headed for the border"

"I think it should be considered Sir" the officer replied.

"Very well, send a team to check out the road, especially the junction you just indicated, but have the dogs start their search where you found the parachutes, they'd got a three hour start" he took a pack of cigarettes out of his breast pocket, took one out of the pack lit it using his lighter and took a long 'drag' before continuing, "that means they're at least fifteen miles away now, maybe as much as thirty depending on how fit they are!"

"You think sir?" the officer was somewhat younger than he was.

"These aren't your average mercenaries" Gregorovitch replied, "They're super fit and superbly trained!" he continued looking at the map; he was thinking just how to beat them. "I want them alive so that we can find out who sent them! And here's how we're going to do it!" he took the map from the wall and clearing the table, taking a pencil he marked two spots on the map. "Here's where the parachutes are" he said, "and here's where the vehicle was last seen, my guess is the vehicle will continue down this road and meet up with the parachutists somewhere around here." He pointed to a junction in the road somewhere about thirty miles from Alamut, "From there they'll strike out for the border using the back roads!"

"So how do we stop them?" the officer was curious and a little dubious as to what the plan might be,

"Simple" Gregorovitch looked up and replied, "We divide and conquer!" He drew circles round the marks, "we keep the two separate and take them down separately! The Iranians have all the roads blocked and roving patrols will keep the mobile team's heads down so we concentrate on taking down the parachutists!"

"Sounds like a good plan" the other officer liked it.

"I want the Hind to deploy the hounds here" he pointed to the spot where the parachutes had been found, "that way, either way, they've gone we'll know as the dogs' noses don't lie, and we'll be able to cover a lot of ground very quickly"

"As soon as we've got a direction from the dogs we'll seal all the roads off down that path, they've got about three hours head start, so I think they've covered at least twenty miles" He stopped and thought for a moment, then continued. "Let the Iranians go after the vehicle with roadblocks and village searches, we'll concentrate on these two". He smiled slightly, "and when we catch them, God help them, because I'm going to make them pay, then I'll extract the information, and then, when we're finished killing it'll seem we're being merciful"

Chapter 14

Joey and Sandy kept going for the whole morning and most of the afternoon in which they made another twenty miles, but the noise from behind them was steadily getting louder and louder as they heard the sounds of men and hounds pursuing them.

They kept to the remote parts of the mountains as much as they could, but even here there were villages and with every village, they came across the chances of capture grew exponentially as more and more people joined the search.

Word had gotten out among the villagers, and whatever they were being told had put them firmly on the side of the pursuers with each village sending out their own search parties and effectively keeping Joey and Sandy away from any of the villages, thus forcing them into the remote regions and into one valley, it was starting to get uncomfortable as it felt as if they were being driven into a trap, like a noose slowly being tightened around their necks.

"Let's stop here for a moment" Sandy was beginning to tire, she'd kept up all the way so far, but the level of fitness between the two was beginning to show. She sat down on a rock overlooking the oncoming valley; they'd managed to take to the saddle of a ridge, getting a view of what's ahead and who's behind them. "How far back do you think?" she didn't finish the question.

"Still about three miles or so I'd say" Joey replied, "We'll have to deal with them soon though"

"Yeah" she replied, neither of them were looking forward to it, a showdown against Spetznaz and the foreign legion wasn't something to look forward to, even if you had superior numbers and the advantage, they had neither!"

It was then they heard a faint noise in the distance, low and hardly detectable to the normal ear, but the senses were still on 'overdrive' and they heard something, a kind of like a massive diesel engine growling with fury as it pushed a heavy load up a mountain. "Is that what I think it is?" Joey began.

"A train? Wait a minute, I think we are near a rail line" Sandy made a grab their map, "Yeah look, the other side of this mountain" she pointed to the one on their left, "The line runs down from Tehran but turns east-west just ten miles back, it runs all the way to the border, or pretty close to it!" she looked up, "and I think it's only about two miles from here!"

"Then we've got work to do"

Jacko had a different solution to their problem, they were going to 'go looking' for the enemy! But not yet, at the right time they'd do an 'advance to contact' as it was known. If the Iranians were setting up roadblocks on the main roads with the major convoys then it was only a matter of time before they sent smaller units down the back roads to begin the search between the villages, or better yet send units to mobilize the villagers into searching, they'd keep going, keep heading west until they met such a unit, then they wouldn't hesitate, they'd go 'head to head with the whole damn republican guard if they had to!

"We'll need to be about ten miles from the main road" Jacko spoke to the team, "Then they'll be too far to call up for assistance" he pulled the vehicle over as they came into sight of the first village, driving straight through the village would be risky, it would draw the locals attention to them who might notify the Iranians as to where they were and would take the element of surprise away from them, but skirting the village was going to take time, and that was a commodity they just didn't have.

"Boss" It was Smithy who spoke, "It's close to the morning prayer time, if we wait until then most of the village will be praying or out in the fields, we could drive through then and it's likely they'll just think we're foreigners from the fortress!" he had a point, about the only thing they could do and one worth taking a risk on, besides that few minutes wait would give them time to check a few things out like Mac's wound which they could see he was in pain with but there's no way he'd ever admit it.

Mac's wound was checked, the dressing was holding and no fresh blood seeping through, once a field dressing is on then the only time you take it off is when the Doctor is going to patch the wound up, "Sorry Mac" Jacko looked directly at him, "We can't give much for pain relief!" They did have Morphine but that would mean Mac being high as a kite and that was the last thing needed, they needed everyone fully alert and functional, Mac was alert, functional but it pain and doing a bad job of trying to hide it. His only reply was "I bloody well told ye! It's only a flaming scratch"

The prayer call began and they saw a couple of men making their way to the village Mosque, the women were either in the fields with their men or in the homes making food for the evening meals.

"Time to move folks" Jacko spoke softly as he put the 'cruiser' into gear they drove into the village watching every home they passed for signs of trouble.

The average home in this part of the world is more like a mini fortress; a five-foot high wall surrounds a courtyard where the women do their work of cooking and cleaning, at the back of the 'compound' is a two-room building built of mud brick, one is where the people sleep and the other is where everyone eats, that is if there are no visitors, usually there are and that means it's where the men eat with the women having their own eating place in the courtyard.

The team got through the village without incident and as far as they could tell without being spotted, at least no one was following screaming for their blood.

Outside the village the trees cleared somewhat as the road took a left turn and headed round the mountain, climbing as the village receded into the distance, just before the road crossed the skyline they head the noise they were all dreading.

About a mile away heading from the north to the south at high speed the Hind was really moving, it didn't stop, but there was no way they couldn't have been seen.

"Oh Shit" was all anyone could say, but it was Chambers who voiced what everyone was thinking.

"Big fella in the sky" It was Smithy who spoke up, kind of praying in his own inimitable way. "I know we don't talk that often, but hopefully you're not too pissed off with me for that and might consider this little request" he went on, "Joey's probably on the receiving end of that lot" he pointed to the weapons pods they could see on the aircraft, "Keep him safe as he's a mate Lord, can you? Thanks" not exactly the pattern for prayer you're taught in Sunday school but Smithy was sure God wasn't too fussed about patterns so much as listening when you call or scream out, 'he just likes it when you talk to him' was Smithy's reply. They all replied, "Amen to that".

"Think they saw us?" It was Chambers asked the obvious,

"I'd lay money on it" Jacko replied in a 'matter of fact' tone. "So let's get the hell out of here before the reception committee show up"

Chapter 15

"Sir" It was Konrad, his second in command speaking to him. "We just got a call from the second Helicopter asking if we have any vehicles in the valley to the west of the fortress."

"What? No of course not! Why?" Gregorovitch was almost impatient, "Why?"

"Because they just spotted a black Landcruiser on the far side of the valley wall here" he pointed to a location about forty miles west of the fortress, a long way from where they thought the RV would be, but still within the search area that the Iranians were searching. "He wants to know if he should engage."

Gregorovitch spent a few moments looking at the map, could they be making a dash for the border? It was possible, but how sure could they be. "How sure is he that's they're the people we're looking for?"

Konrad replied almost immediately, "How many more black Landcruisers do you know of in Iran? They're all white ones!"

"Good point" Gregorovitch replied, "How many in the vehicle?"

"Pilot couldn't say sir" Konrad replied, "it was only a fleeting image as they were going down the valley"

The Helicopter was another Hind and was en route from Tabriz into the area with extra bodies for the search and to provide extra firepower when they finally cornered the 'terrorists'.

"Tell the pilot stay on course" Gregorovitch moved back to the map, he placed a pin on the map at the location the pilot had reported, "Call the Iranians and report what the pilot told you, that way they'll get some credit and feel better about themselves when they take these people down, meanwhile we'll concentrate on the ones that got away on foot, how far away are the dog teams from them now?"

They're catching them sir, they should have them within the hour"

"Good, we'll need all the firepower when we do" Gregorovitch moved away from the map and headed for the coffee pot on the small burner on a table at the back of the new command post, he poured himself a black coffee with no sugar. "Let me know when we have them within sight" and with that, he reached into his pocket, took out a pack of cigarettes and headed for the door.

Just at the door, he stopped, "On second thoughts" he said, "How long until the Iranians get there?"

"About half an hour sir"

"Have the Helicopter make a pass and immobilize the vehicle, then we can send the Iranians in to sort out any stragglers"

Chapter 16

There were nine of them in the unit. Eight foreigners and one local translator, though the translator was from Tehran and only spoke Farsi and not the local Kurdish, still they were functional and had got the information to do what they needed from the villagers.

Two dog handlers with large dogs, German shepherd dogs specially trained for hunting people in rough terrain, the dogs were in the lead and making it obvious they had Joey and Sandy's scent; they were hot on the trail and gaining fast.

"They went this way" it was the lead handler encouraging the others in the group to get a move on; he loved the chase and loved what he did. "Come on, shift your idle arses" he was screaming at the others as they came into the small gulley.

The secret of any ambush is total surprise. That might sound obvious but you'd be amazed at how many times we seem to forget this and set up a half prepared ambush then expect it to 'work like clockwork' yet it can't! When you are going to ambush a force superior in number to yourself there's an added proviso that you really need to make sure of. Hit them with a massive amount of firepower!

Sounds simple right? The massive firepower is simply the 'equalizer' as you cut the force down to a manageable size.

It actually sounds so much easier than it really is! The whole thing relies on timing, get the timing wrong and the first volley goes in before you're ready and the enemy has the time to recover meaning they are ready for you when the attack finally happens, some of the biggest screw-ups in history were because the timing was wrong!

Joey and Sandy were behind boulders about seventy yards to the right of the track, hidden and waiting for the signal, "You won't be able to miss it" Joey'd said as he got into position.

The dogs were in the lead, each one was on a leash literally 'dragging' their handlers along almost at a full sprint, they had the scent and were following it, that was the plan that Joey'd explained hurriedly why he wanted him and Sandy to go through the trap and move about two hundred yards down the track before moving off to the right and back to boulders, they were upwind of the group so there was little chance of their plan being 'rumbled' but you just can't be too careful.

The dogs saw the wires, they were at human ankle height so they simply stepped over them and carried on, barking as they went, the humans don't speak 'dog' and didn't pick up on the warning, they didn't see the wires, they also didn't hear the small click as pins were pulled from their housing and grenade arms dropped onto the soft foliage on the ground.

The average hand grenade has a short time delay fuse of between three point six and five point five seconds, not quite the same fuse in every 'grenade' but enough to give the thrower enough time to 'get out of the way' by throwing it or simply ducking. Joey and Sandy didn't need that, but they still had their 'signal' they were waiting for.

The gulley erupted in a series of violent and deadly explosions; six hand grenades going off all within a second of each other, of the nine men in the pursuit group three were killed instantly, dead before they hit the ground. Two more slumped to the floor clutching their stomachs and screaming, they sounded almost inhuman; it was obvious they weren't going to last long. That left four more.

Joey and Sandy both broke cover at the same time "Shoot anyone that moves" Joey's orders had been, they both had their weapons set on 'double shot' that allowed two shots to be fired with a single pull of the trigger, "Aim for the torso" Joey'd said, "that way when the rifle pulls upwards, you'll get one in the torso and one to the head"

"Why?"

"The one in the torso should kill them" Joey explained. "But the one to the head makes totally sure! And besides, it's SAS practice" he explained, "You do that and they'll know they're dealing with a deadly enemy!"

Both of them ran towards the rest screaming and firing as they went, the trackers were deafened and confused, in no shape to return fire.

Sandy aimed and fired in the general direction, one went down instantly, Joey'd put his man down and was moving on to the next who was starting to reach for his weapon, a quick burst from the commando took care of him, blowing him clean off his feet and sending him sprawling about six feet before crashing into the ground, a second burst left him unrecognizable with no face.

Sandy's second man almost had his rifle in the firing position, it was him or her, she didn't hesitate, screaming at the top of her voice the volley tore into his torso pinning him to a tree before slumping down, she moved forward and let fly with two more rounds into the head.

"Sandy, Sandy" it was Joey's voice she recognized. "Was he hit?" she began to panic, then she realized what he was saying "They're all down now, we can stop" it took a moment for it to register, they'd just taken down odds of five to one against with a ruthlessness she didn't know she had and it shocked her.

"Remember" Joey spoke quietly, almost comforting, "it was them or us, if they'd pulled the ambush off they would be just as ruthless and deadly, they wouldn't have given us a chance either!" he reached out and gently lowered her gun barrel that was pointing in his general direction, "Now let's check and make sure" he cocked his commando and walked round the group putting a shot through each one's skull to make sure there were no nasty surprises.

The last part of the deal was when he came to the dogs, one was clearly dead, having taken a chest of shrapnel, but the other was seemingly unharmed, standing there trembling with fright and shock the animal urinated where he stood as Joey approached, he was terrified, and trying so hard to get away, but the dead hand of his handler was holding him firm, the dog was dragging the dead weight of the body in an effort to get away from the inevitable.

Joey just couldn't do it, he'd grown up with animals and in many ways, they'd been better friends to him than the humans in his life. He slowly advanced towards the frightened beast shouldering his rifle and extending his arm in a friendly gesture, "We're taking the dog with us" he spoke out loud.

Sandy stopped in her tracks; she'd been gathering the weapons up and stripping them down to throw the

firing pins away, denying the enemy the use of the
weapons and had accepted that Joey would kill the dog,
not that she liked the idea, but you have to be ruthless in
this world, "What?" was all she could say.

"We're taking the dog" Joey replied, "we can't
leave him here, they'll use him to track us again".

"I know that," she said, "but why not just kill it?"

"It's not an 'IT'" he said "he's a male! And don't
ask me to kill him, as I'm not going to do it"

Sandy was stunned and relieved as she too was an
animal person, but she still had to know why "Mind me
asking what the difference is? Between the men and the
Dog?"

"They chose to be here" Joey's voice was full of
contempt, not for her but for the men they'd killed here,
"This dog didn't have a choice! So we're taking him with
us" that was it, neither of them wanted to argue with the
irrational decision; it just felt right, that's what they'd do.
"We'll get to the border and then find him a villager to
look after him as a working dog, but we're not killing him
and that's bloody final"

Sandy had no intention of arguing with him, but
something in the tone told her that this was more than a
'tactical decision' this was personal for Joey and it really
spoke volumes to the woman, that this highly trained
'soldier' had a part of him that he just wouldn't allow the
horror of the present situation to 'break into' no matter
how horrible things seemed to be and how illogical it
made things seem, there were some things within Joey that
were 'off limits' to even the Army, not something she
expected.

The drive was not without its little problems, but they seemed to be making good time and it looked like the Iranians hadn't yet totally sealed the area off, they made the next junction and were heading for a ravine when Smithy called out.

"Boss, sink the bloody boot on that gas pedal" he screamed. "The sodding Hind is making a pass and she's looking like she's coming for us!"

"Shit" was Jacko's only reply, "Okay boys, when I say, jump for it" they all grabbed the handles of the doors.

The secret of jumping out of a vehicle at high speed is timing and how you land, how you land in that you'll need to roll over and over to gradually slow your momentum and timing as if you hit a post in the process it doesn't matter how much you roll you're going to die as the impact will break just about every bone in the body!

"Now" Jacko screamed just as they passed the last open ground before the ravine, four doors flew open and four bodies went tumbling hands covering their heads and pulling them as far into their bodies as they could possibly get them in, right at that moment they heard a whoosh as two rockets passed them and impacted on the side of the ravine showering them with debris, the vehicle continued on down the track in a straight line for a while, then the cannon on the Hind opened up and they saw nothing but rock splinters and dirt, then the explosion told them what they didn't want to know. They were walking from here!

"Stay where you are" Jacko spoke into the mike more for Chambers benefit than anyone else's no one moved as the Hind did one more pass, playing dead might just work and the helicopter might just back off.

"Target destroyed sir" Konrad held one hand over the mike, he'd just taken the call from the pilot reporting the destruction of the Landcruiser, "Pilot thinks no one survived" he reported.

"Good" Gregorovitch replied, "But we'll send the Iranians to confirm that" he looked back at the map "Now what's happening with the dog unit?"

Konrad was on the radio ordering the Iranian units they'd been loaned into the area in a pattern search "Be advised the terrorists are armed and dangerous. Yes they are possibly wounded, but still to be considered dangerous"

"What's the news from the dog unit?"

"Just checking now sir, they haven't reported in for about fifteen minutes"

"Is that normal?"

"Yes sir" Konrad replied, "They're due to check in every half hour, so we've got another fifteen minutes before they check in."

"Any chance we can raise them before then?"

"Maybe, but it depends on the terrain and whether they're listening in"

"Then try, and keep trying until you hear from them" Gregorovitch was looking at the map. "Things are going a little too well at the moment, let's keep them that way"

Chapter 17

"Anyone hurt?" probably one of the dumbest questions you could ask after having to dive from a moving vehicle with rocks fast approaching and a heavily armed helicopter unleashing a salvo of rockets right 'up your arse' but Jacko had to ask the question.

"Apart from my pride, no" Smithy was the first to reply.

"I think I might have broken my arm" Chambers replied next, he sat up holding his left arm delicately, it was injured and would require a sling, but not too serious.

"What about you Mac?" Mac hadn't replied. Jacko sat up and began to look around.

"Sorry boss" Mac finally spoke up, "Must have taken a knock to the head, I was out for a moment there!"

"You mean your head hit the earth and there wasn't an earthquake?" Smithy quipped, "Anything that hits your head usually comes off worst!"

"Anyone see where the chopper is?"

"Nah, sorry boss" Mac replied, "I was out cold, what about you Smithy?"

"He did one pass and then cleared off" It was Chambers who replied, "took off to the south, my guess is he got orders not to worry about us once the 'cruiser' was immobilised"

They looked at the smouldering wreck that had once been the Landcruiser.

"Suppose that means we're flaming well walking the rest of the way then?" It was Smithy who spoke.

"Check your weapons folks" Jacko ordered, "and make ready" he started inspecting his own weapons for damage, "as I think we're going to have company pretty soon, and we'll give them a welcome they're not going to forget in a hurry"

"Any word from the dog unit yet?" Gregorovitch was speaking over the handheld Motorola, he'd set off not long after the last conversation with Konrad in a borrowed helicopter an old French four-seater with twin engines, he was so wanting to be there when they took the group fleeing by foot down he was too impatient to wait for reports.

"Not yet sir" Konrad replied over the radio, "They're half an hour overdue, I've been trying for the last forty-five minutes" he continued. "I'm about to send another team to their last reported location and take it from there!"

"Keep me posted on that" Gregorovitch replied, "We'll be at the search base camp in about fifteen minutes ourselves"

The 'search base camp' was where he was assembling the teams for the takedown. Three teams, one for each possible avenue that the group might have taken, and also one each for setting the ambush, one for cutting the head off, one for closing the route back and finally one for taking out the actual team, there'd be no escape.

They could hear the engines labouring hard as they pushed the freight slowly up the gradient, they finally got to see their transport just as they reached the track, the train was still a ways behind them, but even with the effort of pushing twenty-five thousand tons up the mountain the two massive diesel engines were travelling at about 10 miles an hour it was going to gain on them fast.

"Come on" Joey yelled as he started to run as fast as he could for the train. "This is our ride"

"Right with you" Sandy shouted as she sprinted for the train, they were both carrying their weapons slung around their torsos, neither of them even thought of leaving them behind despite the fact it was about thirty extra pounds in weight.

Two massive diesels, together pulling an assortment of chemical tanks and sealed containers. Three hundred tons of pulling power struggling with about a hundred or so tanks and containers each between twenty to forty tons. The whole lot were loaded onto flatbed railway carriages making it that little bit easier for them to attempt the climb.

Joey got level with one and managed to launch himself on to the deck, grabbing hold of one of the support struts of the tanks he hauled himself up and quickly turned. Sandy was running alongside, her arm outstretched, he reached out and grabbed hold, then she jumped at the same time that he 'yanked' her up onto the deck.

'Sniff' was already on the deck; he'd had no problem catching the train and was stood there licking both of them as they embraced each other.

"Shit, that was one hell of a run" Joey was the one to break the silence, he didn't want to break the embrace but they needed to get things sorted out.

"Yeah" Sandy replied softly, she looked directly into his eyes, then reached up and gave him a kiss, just a small one, but on the lips. "Thank you" was all she said.

For a few seconds, it was as if the world disappeared and there was just to two of them, but then reality came crashing back as they took stock of the situation.

The rear flatbeds had forty-foot containers at the front with the name of MAERSK line stencilled on it and a chemical tank with liquid oxygen at the back.

The tank had enough clearance that they could crawl through between the two.

Sandy went first; sniffer was right beside her having decided she was probably friendlier than Joey. Joey came through last.

The container had four padlocks, heavy duty ones that would deter all except the most determined of thieves. Sandy paused for a moment then taking the backpack off she hunted for a small purse. As soon as she had what she wanted and she set to work.

Less than two minutes later the last padlock popped open, Joey worked the levers and opened the container.

It was like opening the door to Aladdin's cave! About two feet inside the container were pallets, two wide and two high pallets of tinned food, wrapped in cellophane it was just what they needed.

Joey took his knife out of its sheath and began hacking into the cellophane on the left-hand pallet.

"Can't read the label" he said pointing to the Farsi writing, "but it looks like Beef" there was a picture of a cow on the front. In English there was 'Product of Pakistan' written, "wonder if that's really true?" he asked no one in particular. "Not that it matters that much"

The meat had a little key on the side and a lip. He placed the key in the lip and began to turn peeling back part of the tin.

"Here you are Sniff" Joey shook the tin so the meat dropped out onto the floor, sniff didn't wait for Joey to stop, he literally 'inhaled' the food in about two seconds, the tail came from between the legs and showed the slightest hint of a wag, Joey did the same with another tin that Sniff took about a second more to eat, 'When were you last fed?' Joey thought to himself.

"I'd say at least a week ago by the way he ate that!" it was as if Sandy had read his thoughts, she took one of the tins and opened it herself, she ate half the tin then gave the rest to sniff, the tail wagged that little more. Meanwhile, Joey looked round the rest of the container and found tins of Apricots and lentils; he threw one tin of the Apricots to Sandy who promptly opened it.

"Better than a meal at the Savoy," he said!

"Don't know" Sandy replied as she tucked into the Apricots, "But if we get out of this you can take me there and we'll check it out, I'm sure Gordon Ramsay will appreciate that his food's coming second best to tins of raw food stolen from an Iranian goods train!"

"What do you mean IF?" Joey replied with a smile, pretending to be indignant, "of course we're going to get out, and you're on!" he looked directly at her, that brought a smile to her face, though it wasn't sure if it was his confidence or the fact that someone else was paying for a meal at one of the world's top restaurants, one of THE places to eat in London that caused the smile, he liked to think it was his wonderful charm, the thought that she

actually earned more than three times what he did never
entered his head.

Chapter 18

"We've probably got about half an hour before
they show up" Jacko spoke slowly; they could see he was
formulating a plan.
"Enough time to bug out boss?" Mac asked.

"Or arrange a welcoming party" Jacko replied, "I
don't fancy walking out of here, and our chances wouldn't
be that great, how about we get ourselves some transport?"

"You mean 'borrow' a vehicle like we did the
cruiser, sounds good to me" Smithy was up for it.

Most places talk about their staff being a 'great
asset' and then the bosses make decisions like their staff
don't matter, not Special Forces! Especially not the SAS,
their decisions are always done by a vote, that way men
and women with years of experience have input 'all the
way' and everyone 'owns it' and when your back's literally
against the wall with nowhere to go that's exactly what
you need.

"We'll try not to kill any this time, as the last thing
we need is to make an even worse enemy of the Iranians"
Jacko spoke for the group, the plan was 'high risk and they
all knew it. "I reckon it's going to take about half an hour

for anyone to show, time enough for you to get a good position Smithy"

As the best shot in the unit it was going to be his job to make sure that the unit that walks into the ambush stayed there and stayed isolated, he walked down the gulley about a hundred and fifty yards then found a place with good cover that gave him a good view of both the approach and the 'kill zone' then set down to wait.

The rest of the plan was simple, Chambers and Mac were both injured, though neither was all that serious, they'd taken a few moments to put Chamber's arm in a sling and the dressing on Macs wound was holding with no blood seeping through, you could see he was in pain, but not enough to hinder what he had to do, and that was to play dead.

Mac climbed into the burned-out wreck of the vehicle, he sat in what was left of the driver's seat, the lack of charring on his body would probably give the ambush away to the wary, but they were counting on the Iranians being unwary and not expecting anything, Chambers sprawled out in front of the cruiser as if thrown clear in the blast. Mac had his Glock out and Chambers had a Makarov they'd picked off one of the dead back at the fortress, Jacko took up a position near the burned-out vehicle, no sooner had they got into position than they heard what they were waiting for.

"Boss" it was Smithy, "Our friends have arrived with the transport"

"Good, now to persuade them to let us have it" Jacko replied. "Smithy, we move on your signal"

"Agreed" they all replied one by one and the radio went silent, no one needed to speak, they all knew what to do.

The 'Transport' was a sort of Humvee, in that it was an All Terrain Vehicle but looked more like a Landrover with a fifty calibre mounted on the roof and a tandem axle at the back, there was a soldier in the hatch manning the fifty cal, neutralizing that was Smithy's job.

The vehicle stopped about fifteen yards short of the burned out hulk and two men got out, one officer and another soldier covering the officer's moves, there were a couple of others in the back of the vehicle, they stayed in the vehicle.

"On your mark Smithy" Jacko spoke quietly, he probably didn't need to, but no one argued.

"Roger boss" Smithy came back, "wait until he's checking the bodies"

The officer moved forward and headed for the body in the vehicle first, the soldier moved round to get a clear bead on the body unencumbered by the officer, he stepped over Chambers and stopped just in front of him, he raised his rifle into the ready position, ready but slightly relaxed.

A dull thud was heard and the soldier at the fifty cal slumped forward screaming as he grasped for his shoulder.

All hell broke loose as Chambers scissor kicked the supporting soldier making contact between the legs, he fell to the floor as Chambers jumped up and grabbed the Kalashnikov out of his hands, he levelled the Makarov at the soldier, "DON'T MOVE" he screamed in Farsi.

Mac spun round and levelled the Glock at the officer who was reaching for his pistol, "DON'T BE SO BLOODY STUPID!!" he screamed in his broad Glaswegian English but it was plain what the meaning was.

Jacko sprinted for the vehicle, flung open the driver's door and yanked the driver out of his seat before he had time to think about what he was seeing, the driver ended up in a heap on the floor, he came too with a Colt Commando levelled at his head they all raised their hands and began to pray like crazy in their own language and under their breath, a quick jerk of the commando told the rest of them where to go, move to the front and don't do anything stupid! Slowly and deliberately they moved with their hands behind their heads, the slightest twitch, well no one wanted to find out what would happen as it clearly wasn't good for the Iranians.

The officer had his pistol, a Chinese 'knockoff' of the more reliable Makarov out of his holster, kind of a reflex action when he realized it really wasn't a good idea. He holstered it, raised his hands and told his men to do the same.

None of them wanted to die, so they all did as they were told and raised their hands. Jacko indicated where he wanted them; he also indicated them to take their boots off. Meanwhile, Steve was busy relieving them of all their weapons and ammunition. The ammo would come in handy and replace any they'd used but they took the firing pins out of the weapons, they didn't want to have to deal with these 'clowns' again.

"Any of you speak English?" Jacko asked as Chambers moved round the back of each Prisoner, he'd finished dismantling the weapons and had found some Ziploc ties intended for securing prisoners, that was exactly what they were going to be used for, except not the prisoners they were meant for.

"A little" one of the soldiers, a very nervous looking corporal replied.

"Tell your officer I have a message for your General" Jacko paused for him to translate, as soon as he stopped speaking Jacko went on, "We're not 'terrorists' or murderers" he paused while the soldier translated, "that's the reason you're being spared, but the people you are working with are!" Jacko carried on, "Those men in the fortress at Alamut planted the bombs in Istanbul, using them to kidnap a British diplomat, and they killed so many just to get at that diplomat, surely they must have known we'd retaliate!" he paused for the man translating to catch up.

"We have no quarrel with the people of Iran" Jacko started off again, "but if you try to stop us from reaching safety make no mistake, we will not hesitate, DO YOU UNDERSTAND?" he shouted the last part, all the prisoners rocked back at the ferocity he used. They understood all too well!

They were trussed up and going nowhere, but Jacko wasn't finished, "We'll leave you some water and supplies further down the road so that you can get out of here, but we're taking the transport." He stopped and turned back to the soldier, "make sure your General gets the message" then he turned back to the vehicle, "Okay boys let's mount up"

The sun was descending over the Western mountains as they entered the tunnel. They were still in the container but had pulled the doors so that to the casual observer they looked as if they were closed

Joey told Sandy to "get some shut-eye" as they'd need to be rested up when they left the train; it was going to be a long hard run for the border. He spent the time cleaning and checking the weapons, they'd used about a magazine each from the Commando and the Kalashnikov, but they'd been able to restock the AK so things weren't too bad, they were in a good situation with the ammunition.

Grenades were a slightly different story, Joey'd used six grenades in the trap and was down to only two left, but he still had a full load for the grenade launcher.

Squealing from the tracks was what told him they were slowing down, the train was applying the brakes, and not sure if there were any signals that they were obeying he decided to get ready for the worst.

"Time to get off" Joey shook Sandy back awake, she'd dozed off for about a half hour, it'd felt good to have even that short sleep. "We're getting close to the border"

"Where are we exactly?" Sandy took a moment or two to come around; they were still inside the container and had closed the doors.

"We've been on the train an hour or so" Joey replied. "We were sixty miles from the border when we boarded, so I reckon that makes us about ten to fifteen miles from the border and near to the rail yards where customs check the freight before sending it into Iraq"

"So why not stay on?" Sandy thought 'surely if the train's going into Iraq it makes sense to stay onboard'

"Customs" Joey replied without a hint of a rebuke, "You can bet a pound to a pinch of salt they'll be checking for us, as well as all the other stuff they check for! Besides, I think they just stopped the train for a specific search, before Customs gets here if you know what I mean!"

It was Sniffer who alerted them. One minute he was fairly relaxed, the next he was alert, ears pricked up, hair on his back rising and letting out a low growl.

Joey took hold of his harness and gently got sniffer to lie down, he managed to cover the dog's snout and stop him growling or barking. They'd heard nothing, but a dogs hearing is so much more sensitive than a human's, whatever he heard can't be good.

As Joey was getting sniffer to relax, he'd done his job. Sandy slowly opened the container doors, there was just enough light to see the tunnel.

"They're searching the train" her voice was just above a whisper. "Still a ways up near the front, but they're checking everything"

"They'll have the exit covered for sure" Joey answered her unasked question, "we'll have to think some other way, meanwhile we can't stay in here.

Just then Sandy whispered " I've got an idea but we'll have to move fast, come on get a move on" she grabbed the padlocks and handed two to Joey, "you clip the top two on, I'll do the bottom two"

Seconds later they were out, the compartment closed and they were moving.

Chapter 19

They were totally still, not daring to move even the slightest finger as the searchers marched past. Even sniffer seemed to understand that movement now would result in instant death at the hands of merciless men, not that he liked Joey holding his snout so tightly; they could still hear the occasional low growl in protest.

They'd just had enough time to lock the container and climb back under one of the oxygen tanks as the searchers made their way methodically along the train, both of them had their weapons at the ready but reality was in a situation like this it really was a last resort as death for all would be almost certain.

The searchers were speaking mainly Russian, but some rattled off in German occasionally, usually a cuss at their commander, a guy called Gregorovitch, Sandy recognised the name, Joey looked at her inquisitively but she made a gesture that said "Later"

Two of the searchers drew level with the tank they were hiding under, Joey shrank back even further into the shadows, unseen yet watching every move, ready to react and try to give Sandy the best possible chance, though even that wouldn't be all that great in the situation.

"Nothing here" he heard one voice say in German, his German was passable, everyone in the Army spends time in Germany and learns at least a smattering of the language, at least enough to order a 'Beer and Fries' if nothing else! "I suppose those arseholes in charge got it wrong AGAIN!" the voice continued, they heard faint agreements down the line and some laughter at other comments he couldn't quite make out. He could see Sandy's face, she was smiling too, but it seemed she understood German as well!

'Like looking for a needle in a bloody haystack' was Gregorovitch's thought, actually it was more like a needle in a very dry haystack using a naked flame to light up what you're seeing, a recipe for disaster if you didn't know what you were doing, but you don't get to be a senior Spetznaz officer by not knowing what to do! And he had the perfect plan, it just needed the right 'magnet' and that was simple, the idea they might actually get away with it.

"Sir" Konrad spoke as Gregorovitch entered the command post, "The teams have checked the train in the tunnel, and they didn't find anyone!"

"I didn't expect them to!" Gregorovitch replied he'd seen the carnage Joey and Sandy had inflicted on his search team. All nine had been killed, and it was done with a ruthless efficiency that told him volumes about the attackers. "But they're there, and they're too smart to show themselves"

"Do you want to order another search of the train?"

"No, let's back off for now" he was thinking, "Even if we find them, in that tunnel, with a confined space like that it'd be a disaster."

Searching 'confined spaces like a tunnel is always a 'trade off' with risk and necessity, risk in that the 'hunter' is often more than the 'hunted' so you have the numerical advantage, but there's also a restricted area where the bullets can fly and that means the hunter is presenting more targets than the hunted, not only that but it's often the 'prey' that's got the drop on the 'hunter!'

Effectively the 'hunter' becomes the hunted by sheer stupidity!

"We'll back off for now" Gregorovitch continued, "but we'll keep an eye on the train and watch what happens when it comes out of the tunnel," he stared for a moment at the map on the wall, then continuing he said. "They've got to make a break for it somewhere, and I think I know the place they'll do it" he pointed to the map, "Right here!"

"It looks ideal sir!" Konrad looked on approvingly. The 'map' was actually a satellite image of the area and showed a clear flat piece of land about a mile wide and half a mile across with the mountains hemming it in to the North, East and South but the west, a river ran through it, the border was the river, there wasn't even a bridge there as it was meant to be mined with anti-personnel mines from one or more of the many wars in the area, at least that's what the reports said!

"How sure are we about the mines in the area sir?" Konrad wanted to know.

"The data's old" Gregorovitch replied, "But we're not going to rely on that, have a couple of spotters placed on the train, make sure they understand we need to know exactly when these scum debus the train and where they're going" he paused for a moment, then went on. "The rest of the teams we'll place here, as soon as we get an idea we'll close the trap and finish this!" he gave an evil smile that said it all, no mercy would be given!

The ATV turned out to be a Chinese 'knockoff' of the American Humvee, right down to the armour plating on the floors against IED's that'd proved so devastating in Iraq and Afghanistan, the motor didn't quite have the acceleration the American ones had, but it had some serious 'grunt' for hauling heavy loads over the rough terrain they were travelling, and the serious firepower they had 'up top' was some heavy equipment.

"Smithy" Jacko called out above the noise of the cab, "What's our situation with the Ammo?" they knew it had to be good as they could hear the whistling of a man who was very happy, just like an adolescent kid who's just got the fastest motorbike on the block!

"She's a Chinese version of the fifty cal boss" Smithy came back, "and so far I've got two boxes of ammo, both full and unopened, along with the belt that was in the gun, I'd say about three thousand rounds altogether!"

"Shiiiit!!!" it was Chambers let out the expletives, "What were they trying to stop, a team, or an Army?" he looked across at Jacko who was concentrating on the road.

"All they knew was we made a hell of a mess of Alamut!" Jacko replied without taking his eyes off the road, "besides, they may have had all the toys, but they weren't anticipating using them! At least that team wasn't"

"How long you think it'll be before they find out we took their 'toys'?"

"Hard to say really" They were all hoping 'never' but that wasn't the reality, "depends on how long it takes those boys to get free!"

"You honestly think the Iranians will back off?" Mac chirped in.

"Not a chance!" Jacko replied, he'd suggested the idea of sending the message back (and letting the men live) but none of them really thought it would work, the best they thought they'd get out of it was confusion as to why and what purpose, "But we had to try!"

"But those men can be put back in the field!" Chambers pointed out the fallacy.

"Only after a severe bollocking by the C.O. which will waste his time and then having to go back to the armoury which will waste more time and money for the Iranians, by which time it'll be all over!"

Kill an enemy and it takes two men three or four hours to bury him and it's over, but wound or confuse him and it could take ten men months to sort out the mess! The key to winning in their situation was cause havoc and confusion! Cause so much trouble the enemy literally doesn't have a clue where they are and is 'chasing his tail' all over the place long after 'Elvis has left the building' if you know what I mean, that had been the plan with the message!

They were within fifteen miles of the border when Jacko pulled the vehicle over and took out the Satellite phone, there was a pre-arranged number he was to call, let it ring four times and hang up, that was the signal for 'extraction'

Sixty miles away an operator was sitting at the other end when the lights on his display came on, straight away he knew what it was and whom to call, the Officer had explained it to him in detail, he'd also explained that it was to be put through no matter what time of day or night it came in, and "I don't give a shit who you have to cut off!!" was the message he got.

The 'Officer' was colonel Simpson and was actually on the line with Sir Michael when the call cut in, "Sir" the operator began, "Sorry for the interruption but we just got the signal, I'm activating the GPS now"

"Good work man" Simpson replied, "send the word to the Air Corps boys, I want them airborne within minutes"

"They're already running start-ups sir" the operator replied, he'd kicked the pilots out of the Command post before he called the Colonel, it's the kind of thing a lowly corporal doesn't get the chance to do to senior ranks very often, so when opportunity presents itself it has to be taken with gusto, and he'd loved every second of it! "The GPS information will go directly to their onboard navigation computers, they'll get the info mid-air, the Lynx is enroute for you now sir, it'll be there in five"

"Bloody good work man!" the Colonel almost shouted as he ran for the door, he clicked the phone off and ran at the sprint for the helipad, there was no way on earth he was going to miss this, Sir Mike could bloody well wait for the news, at least as long as they were airborne.

Rounding the corner their fears were realised as they came face to face with a checkpoint, a tracked

Armoured Personnel carrier with half a dozen men in, sat at a road checkpoint and about four or five bored frustrated looking guards, the APC was reinforcement for the situation, they hadn't been rumbled yet, but even just approaching the checkpoint meant that discovery was inevitable, and they had to get through.

"You" Jacko looked directly at Chambers, "Head down and sodding well stay that way!" he shouted, there was no time to be nice, "Smithy, on my mark take the APC first, Mac, when he starts" he nodded in Smithy's direction, "Level the guard building, I'll bowl the men in the road, that should get us through at least, then it's all bets are off and we race for the extraction site!"

He approached the checkpoint slowly at first, then about a hundred yards from the barrier he floored the gas pedal and screamed "NOW!"

An ear-shattering roar came from above as Smithy opened up with the fifty cal, the men in and around the APC stood no chance whatsoever as the cannon shells tore limb from limb, at that range the one inch armour plating on the APC gave way to the massive velocity of the shells that ripped through it like a can opener opening a supermarket bean can, and with less resistance. The guard hut was engulfed in a ball of flame as two grenades fired from the grenade launcher exploded taking the whole building out, men were running screaming, diving for the nearest cover, but not sure if that was going to be next. Jacko aimed the vehicle between the roadblocks knowing full well that the barrels in the road were actually concrete 'tank stops' that if he hit them head on they would literally stop them in their tracks and throw the team clear through the windscreen, the only way was to 'bounce' through them with glancing blows, effectively like a bullet ricocheting off them and carrying on through, that was the plan what plan there was that is!

Somehow, by some miracle the 'gods of war' shone down on them that day, and they made it through the whole checkpoint, the Humvee 'knockoff' showed it was almost as tough as the original and made it through almost intact, though they all swore they'd wear seatbelts in future and Jacko was NEVER to be allowed to drive on British roads ever again!

"After that piece of shit boss" Smithy was almost laughing at the fact they got through, a nervous laugh, "I think I'm going to have a word with my mate at the Driving school and see if we can get you some real lessons!"

"Smithy" Jacko replied, "I was going to say if you could do better you're welcome to try, but we damn well need you on that gun! We're going to have company all the way now!"

"Thanks for the heads up boss" Smithy replied, "But they're already mounting up, there were a couple more vehicles hidden and they're pretty pissed!" Just then a huge explosion almost rocked the Humvee, "Did I point out they've got a sodding Scorpion?"

A Scorpion Tank. British built and sold to the Iranians in the late 1970s still the fastest tank ever built with a top speed of over a hundred miles an hour on the test track and over fifty in real combat situations. Armed with a 76mm gun, and a 7.62mm 'ranging' machine gun it was a serious opponent, there was no way they could even think of outrunning the damn thing, but it does have one weakness and that was its armour or lack of it! The

Scorpion's armour plating is only just over an inch thick and made of Aluminium, it relies on its speed as its main defence! In a fast-moving battle that can be a huge advantage, but only if the enemy doesn't know its weakness!

"I'm not going back to deal with that!" Jacko replied. "Any chance you can take her out on the move?"

"There's a depression ahead boss" Smithy shouted a reply just as the machine gun on the tank opened up, they heard the last of the shells as they hit the back of the vehicle, not penetrating as the Kevlar plate protected them, but enough that the gunner in the tank could see he'd got their range. "Get her in there and we can take her as she comes over the rise!" they were going flat out now, Jacko swung the wheel hard right just as they heard the boom of the main gun, the Tank was about two hundred yards behind and closing fast, she was well ahead of the other two Humvees following, they were now less than ten miles from the border. The shell impacted right in the track where they would have been if they'd kept the same course. As soon as the shell landed he jerked the wheel hard left and headed off on a new tangent. Two or three more shells and erratic driving from Jacko was all that kept them from being obliterated, they'd never complain about bad drivers ever again!

They went into the depression just as another shell whistled overhead and exploded about twenty yards in front of them, the shockwave rocking the vehicle, but the weight of the Humvee kept her on the road, all they could do now was wait.

The one weak point for any tank is their underbelly, the underside of the tank only usually has mines to deal with, so the armour plating tends to be that much weaker there, it's the one place that manufacturers feel they can save on weight and still retain the awesome capabilities the tank needs, it also leaves as 'Achilles heel' in that as the tank is climbing out of places it needs to get literally 'half way out' before it'll 'flop' back down, that few seconds is when even the greatest monster is like a beached whale, most tanks have their engines mounted at the back to make sure that vital parts don't get 'taken out' but the Scorpion uses the engine as 'extra protection' for the crew and it's mounted at the front, that's what they needed, it would leave the Scorpion totally helpless, unable to fight back, or even move! That was the plan.

Smithy opened up with the fifty cal, it tore into the 'soft underbelly' of the tank and a couple of shells actually made it into the engine compartment disabling the engine, she was out for the count, unable to move and unable to use her gun, the crew were worse than useless now, the only hope they had was tostay inside the tank and hope for the best.

The three of them let out a huge cheer, all except Smithy who was watching the horizon, "Boss, he called down, I wouldn't get too excited if I was you, the rest of the Humvees are hot on the tail, and there are six more hairy arsed ragheads closing fast! Three at two o'clock and three at ten o'clock!"

"Smithy, you got any good news for a change?" Mac shot back as they got underway again; it was going to be bloody tight making the border.

"Mac" Smithy came back, "You take the two o'clock buggers, I'll deal with the ragheads in the other group, they're about four hundred yards and closing fast. "Any luck on raising our taxi out of here boss?"

"We should be just in range now" Jacko replied. "Let's call the cavalry"

Every vehicle in the Military has a call sign; they're often words that the people in the machines can easily remember in battle. Infantry are called 'India' the reason should be obvious, Tanks are called 'Tango' but the role of the Helicopter squadrons is spotting for both of them, their 'sign' is 'Hawkeye' but a 'Longbow 'attack chopper is only going to have one 'sign'

"Hello all call signs' this is Hawkeye, our friends are taking fire, prepare for hostile extraction" Simpson put the word out to the other two Helicopters.

"Robin hood roger" the first Apache came back, "Guns are live"

"Little John Roger" the other came on the radio, "Hood break left, I'll go right."

"Roger that" Simpson came back on, "Remember, intimidate where possible, don't engage unless fired upon" he flicked the radio back to the frequency that Jacko was on, "India one, this is Hawkeye, we're one minute out"

"Stand by boys" Jacko yelled at the top of his lungs, both Smithy and Mac were fully occupied with engaging the closing vehicles, they were just about a hundred yards away and slightly behind them, the soldiers were jumping out and running into battle formation using fire and movement, the fire wasn't hitting them, but it was keeping their heads down. They were taking fire from two directions. Smithy opened up with the fifty cal again, he'd run out of ammo and taken a couple of seconds to change the ammo belts, the first vehicle erupted in a ball of flame, as well as two of the soldiers keeling over, cut down by the withering hail of fire.

"For heaven's sake" Chambers screamed, "Give me a bloody gun, and let me do something!"

"And have this all for nothing!" Jacko screamed back as skidded the vehicle to a halt, "Not a sodding chance!" he swung the wheel violently to the right, Smithy pivoted to the left and kept firing, "Ready, on my word" he threw the door open.

The 'Border' was actually a river running through the valley. The plain they'd been driving on came to an abrupt end with a twelve to fifteen-foot drop into the river, the real 'line' was actually the actually the drop, it was also the cover the choppers had used to come right in without being seen

From seemingly nowhere three shadows rose up, menacing and deadly in the fading light, three helicopters came out of the ground, two menacing looking monsters with missile and gun pods sprouting from the sides and front, they looked evil, and they were the good guys!

The other helicopter was a little less intimidating, but that was the troopship, they were right on the border. They didn't actually land, as the edge was still technically within Iran, they just hovered about a foot from the edge, technically not breaking the law, but sending a serious 'step out of line and we'll blow the shit out of you message!'

The Iranians didn't know what to do if they continued firing the danger was they'd hit one of the helicopters, that might be okay if they stop the whole thing, but with two whacking great monster gunships there the chances of survival was very small indeed. The best thing was to 'get the hell out of dodge' and screw the officers! One of the men was speaking frantically into the radio; someone didn't like what he was telling them.

Back when the Americans developed the Apache gunships the British were pretty impressed with them and after the first gulf war negotiated to have them built under licence in Britain, the British ones were called the 'Longbow' after the legendary Medieval weapon used by English archers that were the scourge of the Medieval battlefield. The only difference was the Longbow was powered by two Rolls Royce engines and instead of the eight Hellfire missiles these carried six Hellfire missiles and two Sidewinder air to air missiles, they were going to need them.

The chance was there and the team took it, jumping out and running at the sprint, Jacko grabbed Chambers and virtually threw him into the machine, next was Mac, then Smithy was bringing up the rear, making sure that none of the Iranians was trying anything, finally Jacko threw himself in "Go" he screamed, "Get the hell back over the river"

"Roger that" the pilot spoke 'matter of factly into the radio, "On our way"

"Where's Joey?" Simpson didn't bother with formalities; he wanted to get them all home.

"Twenty miles south" Jacko shouted, "he and Sandy are heading for a place called Penjuin with a bunch of Hinds on his tail"

"Jesus Jacko" was all he could say, turned the handle on his radio and spoke quickly, the two 'bows' peeled off and flew south, not rising more than five feet off the ground. "They're on their way."

"Drop the wounded off at the village there" Jacko pointed to the village on the map, "and get me the hell in there!"

"We've got a rover patrol waiting for Chambers there" Simpson replied, "But I'm not sure Mac's going to like being left behind"

"You're right there boss." Mac replied, "remember Colonel, you gave us our dishonourable discharge papers, before we left, so you can shove those orders about leaving my behind right where the sun don't shine!" he actually had a smile on his face, but everyone knew he was deadly serious, the only way he was being left behind was incapacitated or dead, and he wasn't either!

"Guess that decides it then" Jacko wasn't going to argue if he did he might get his way, but he'd pay for it later, and that wasn't something to push.

Simpson kind of loved that attitude, but as a Colonel it was really hard to take a junior rank talking to him like that, even one that wasn't 'in' right at that moment, he swallowed hard, partly to bite his tongue before creating an unnecessary confrontation and partly to stop the chest swelling too far with pride. Pride in knowing that as the C.O. of the regiment he'd fostered the attitude that just doesn't leave a mate behind, no matter how impossible or even suicidal the situation seems, you just don't leave mates behind!

Two minutes later a very much protesting Chambers was bundled out of the helicopter and into an armoured Landrover with a platoon from the 1st Battalion

Parachute regiment waiting to escort him all the way to the secure compound just outside Mosul.

"Let's get this flaming bird in the air and go get our mates" Jacko called out to the pilot, Simpson was going back with the rover patrol as he had a 'debriefing' to carry out.

Chapter 20

Gregorovitch went ballistic, he couldn't believe what he was being told, "What the hell happened?" he screamed down the phone forgetting for the moment that he was talking to one of the most senior commanders in the Iranian Military, one that he'd consistently lied to for the last two days! "Are you complete imbeciles? We gave them to you literally on a silver platter" he was screaming and pacing holding the mobile "All you damn idiots had to do was shoot the pricks! And you couldn't even do that"

"You dare talk to me like that!" the General was still stunned at the venom in Gregorovitch's words, "I could have you thrown in jail!"

"You could General." Gregorovitch replied, "but who the hell else is going to clean your damn messes?" he carried on the rant, "Now give me the full details of what went on!"

The next thirty minutes went by with a series of expletives coming out from Gregorovitch every second sentence as they slowly went through a blow by blow account of what had gone wrong with the Iranians attempt to stop the team getting out of the country.

Gregorovitch was conscious that time was ticking and he desperately needed to know what it was that'd stopped the Iranians killing the team as they crossed the border, the arrival of the helicopters was the real answer.

When the Russians built the Hind the main gunship that the Americans were using was the Huey Cobra, a superb machine in itself, she carried a lethal payload and could take a hell of an amount of punishment, but carried only the eight missiles and no machine gun, she was deadly, but the firepower was limited, and she was slow.

For the replacement they took a 30mm Gatling canon, then built a flying machine with rotors around it, as an afterthought they realized she could carry a pretty decent payload of missiles as well, not as many as the Hind, but she didn't need to carry the eight troops the Hind needed for ground support (the Blackhawks got that job!) and she was a hell of a lot faster, as well as new radar that allowed her to hide behind trees when firing! Two serious opponents! And they were coming for the team!

But would they risk a serious diplomatic row? The Iranians said the Apaches (that's what they thought they were!) had sat right on the edge of the Iraqi side! Would they risk the diplomatic shit that would inevitably fall from great heights if they strayed over the border? Just the smallest miscalculation and the pilots would be in deep shit up to their eyeballs, no way the grey faces in Whitehall or Washington would own up to making that decision, he knew exactly how the politicians and career 'grey faces' would think!

"How far away is the train?" he shouted to his officers.

"Still inside the tunnel" Konrad replied, "Maybe twelve miles from the border, and before you ask, I've got two fire teams taking up positions just inside the border, another three-man team on the train watching for movement and the two Hinds bringing up more teams, the rest are on their way by road, should be there by the time we let the train out of the tunnel!"

Sixty men, plus vehicles and two attack choppers all waiting for the next move, and it was their move, he was going to have 'tighter than a duck's arsehole' as the English would say, but you just never know how things are going to work out until they actually happen.

Chapter 21

What the team didn't hear was the call that Simpson gave to the two 'bows', it was simple and to the point. Cutting out the 'flowery words' it was simply "Folks, we've got two of our people in deep shit over there, get in there and escort them out!"

The two Rolls Royces were well into the 'redline' but then again when you keep your engines in as good a condition that the Army like to you know just how much you can push them, and they were right on the limit, screaming at five feet doing two hundred and thirty miles an hour.

"Sir," the pilot, a young female Sergeant by the name of Jenny Saunders spoke up. "You're aware they're in Iran sir, we might cause a problem for Whitehall?"

"Screw Whitehall!" He'd screamed, he didn't doubt Saunders and her crew had abilities, two tours in Syria showed them more than willing to 'mix it with the big boys' and to be honest he'd heard from her C.O. she was one of the best there is, "You intercept and escort!"

"Roger that sir, we'll be there in twenty minutes" the reply came back as the aircraft set off following the river instead of flying direct 'as the crow flies'

"But it's only twenty miles" Simpson came back, "You should be there in less than ten!"

"We're not carrying 'Mavericks' sir" the pilot came back, "If we go direct, we'll need a couple of 'Mavericks' for their radar"

The 'Maverick' air to surface missile is specially designed to lock on to the radar signal that an enemy sends out from its ground bases and follows them back to their source before the radar has a chance to pick up the aircraft that brought it.

Their course was going to be over mountains and rough terrain that means climbing over the ridges and diving back into the valleys, the valleys wasn't a problem, but climbing over hills meant that they'd be coming onto the Iranians radar and that meant within seconds an F4 phantom or worse a MiG 21 would be screaming after them, even with the sidewinders she didn't want to tangle with a MiG and the Hinds!

Going around the 'long way' meant that yes it would take a couple of minutes longer, but it also meant they'd get in and out while obeying the eleventh commandment, the one God gave to Moses after the first ten were given, the one that simply says "Thou shalt not get caught!"

"Okay Jimmy," She spoke into the internal mikes to her 'crewman' what's our situation.

"We're fully loaded boss" Jimmy, a lance corporal with only a few months experience came back over the radio, he was a bit on the 'inexperienced' side, but had so far proved pretty calm in a bad situation, "Five thousand for the Gatling, full Hellfire rocket pods, the whole nine yards". They hoped that they wouldn't need it; somehow she knew that hope wasn't going to come about!

"The chief fixed the Gatling then?" Jenny asked. The last mission the gun had jammed, that was the last thing they needed. "And don't forget those Sidewinders!"

"Told me he replaced the whole gas return rod and barrel boss" Jimmy replied, "Didn't have time to work out what was needed so he just took the whole bloody lot and replaced it"

The AH 64D Apache is the one helicopter that can go 'toe to toe' with the best of the best of them, the British version is known as the 'Westland AH64D Longbow' and it's like an Apache on steroids, and that's exactly what they'll need to be. The Hind is a great 'chopper' but she's big and bulky, she carries an awesome amount of firepower, but the trade-off is maneuverability and when fully armed she can't actually hover, she takes that few micro-seconds more to make a turn, the Longbow can turn in her own length and hovering, she was designed to do it fully armed, and she's got good Chobham or 'spaced' armour, and shit was she going to need it.

"Hood this is Little John" the radio came to life, it was the other pilot, "Guns are hot, missiles armed"

"Hood roger" Jenny replied, "Let's see if we can find them and bring 'em home"

"Roger that. Little John out". The hunters were about to become the hunted.

Chapter 22

The train was going slowly as they came out of the tunnel; there was something that just wasn't right about the situation. Not something that either of them could say what it was or might be, their instinct was just telling them "Watch your back"

That was a natural reaction, but this was something else, thing were too quiet, there should have been other things happening, even if it was just seeing people in the fields or listening to the sounds, but they just weren't there, it seemed odd!

"I don't like this" Joey was almost whispering as he looked out from where they'd hidden, "looks all clear, come on" he slowly climbed out from under the oxygen tank, they were close to the back and the train was still going uphill so it wasn't moving all that fast, but she was starting to pick up speed.

"We're about nine miles from the border" Joey turned to Sandy, "at the trot, it'll take us about three hours"

The sun was gone and the light was fading fast, but visibility was going to be good. That was going to be good and not so good, good in that they would be able to see where they were going, not so in that so would the enemy and considering there were more of them then it weighed in the enemy's favour!

Sniffer was with them, still on the leash, he was now more confident and had even accepted Joey, to a degree that is, he was running just ahead of them, but with the leash, they were able to keep him under control, they weren't expecting traps! Then again, neither were the Phoenix boys and that was their downfall.

Sniffer stopped dead, then he went slightly to the left and put his nose to the ground, Joey immediately went to ground, unslung the Colt, checked the ammo (he had a full magazine for rounds and full complement of grenades ready, he slowly and silently cocked the weapon, he signalled Sandy to "Make ready". She slowly and silently cocked the AK and made sure the safety was on. They were as ready as they could be.

Joey gave the signal to move, from this time on there's no way they could move quickly, Phoenix had something nasty planned not far ahead.

"They're on the move" a voice came over the radio, Gregorovitch was on the other end waiting for the reports, everything was ready for him, all he needed now was for them to get to the right place, then they'd take them down without mercy! He'd tried to make it so they could capture the attackers, but they'd shown they had no intention of going down without a fight and no intention of being taken alive!

"Wait until I give the word" Gregorovitch spoke into the mike, "everyone holdoff until I give the word"

Just as they moved off, a movement caught Sandy's eye, back further up the train something, maybe someone was getting off.

"Joey, back there" she nodded so slowly he hardly saw it, "next carriage, someone just got off". They'd charged the batteries on the night vision visors, but it was too light to switch them on.

"Shit" he cursed quietly.

"Yep." Sandy agreed. "We're in it up to our necks and it's getting deeper! But that's nothing unusual!" She'd kind of accepted that.

"Can't stay here all night though" Joey slowly rose and actually waved in their direction.

"Are you bloody serious?" Sandy spluttered, she was stunned. "Why not throw them a bloody kiss?"

"Good idea" Joey replied and proceeded to throw a kiss their way. "That'll throw them off their game"

They were meant to be keeping low profiles, but Joey was making it clear he knew they were there! He knew what was going on, for the next five minutes they would have no idea what to do.

They saw what his right hand was doing, but Joey was ambidextrous, they missed what his other hand was doing until they faced the Colt, two spits and they were down.

"Head west, and run hard" Joey shouted as he tugged on sniffers leash, the dog was reluctant to leave, he had a scent.

"What the hell?" Sandy was dumbfounded, "that was one hell of a shot" they weren't dead, but they were down, one holding his leg and what was left of his knee, the other holding his gut, he was in a bad way, they'd get no trouble from that quarter.

"What the hell was that?" Sandy demanded.

"What?"

"The blowing the bloody kiss" she was confused and a little angry at the fact she was a little confused but was making it come over that she was angry at Joey, not that he was too worried, he had other things to worry about.

"Well" Joey replied, "You did tell me to!" He knew she was confused, but the best answer was the most direct.

"And if I told you to go jump in a pile of shit? Would you do that?"

"No" he started to laugh, "but it was a bloody good distraction, that's what I needed" they were moving fast, but not so fast they were out of breath but already out of sight of the two men they just downed.

"Look" Joey began again. "Sniff told us they were waiting out there for us, and"

"How'd you make that out?" She interrupted.

"He picked up a scent, what else was it going to be?" he replied, "then you picked the two 'gophers' getting off the train" he carried on, "they were setting us up for an ambush!"

"So what are we doing now?" Sandy was confused.

"Getting the hell out of the 'kill zone' what else?" he replied.

Every ambush has the same basic structure, there are the scouts who spot the target and make sure the 'target' gets to the right place, and the two on the train were the scouts. Their job is to call the main body when the targets are approaching to make sure that the main body, those who'll actually carry out the ambush are in the right place.

The main body selects a place where they can put down a devastating amount of fire without hitting their own side; the place is called the 'kill zone'. That place should give no cover whatsoever to the target and ideally it should be over within two or three seconds, with everyone dead or wounded, that was Gregorovitch's plan for Joey and Sandy. Lastly, there's the tail-enders, their job was to take out anyone trying to get out by running down the track.

They had no idea what side the ambush was on, but Joey guessed it was probably on the southeast side as that would be the easiest for the ambushers, that meant by running west they were increasing the range the ambushers would have to fire to engage them, making it virtually impossible without breaking cover and that gives the advantage (albeit slight) back to the escapees, it was a gamble, but what the hell, they had no choice!

That was when they heard the shots behind them. Rifle fire, a couple of rounds spat up the earth a couple of feet away to the left, too far for accurate shooting, but just enough to give them something to worry about.

"Take cover in the rocks ahead" Joey yelled as he broke into a sprint, as he drew level with Sandy he grabbed her in the small of her back and increased his pace, she did the same.

The rocks were boulders about the size of a man, they both launched themselves at them from about five feet away, both literally vaulted the boulders and did forward rolls into the gaps behind them,

"You okay?" Joey asked as he came back up, stopping just before the top of the rocks, the last thing they needed was to put the head over the top and get it blown off.

"Yeah" Sandy replied, "Just a couple of scratches from the rocks" she was looking at the back of her hands, "What was that?"

"That was just our average AK from a ways away" Joey replied, "probably too far for accurate shooting, but far enough to kill with a lucky shot!"

"Any idea where they are?" she was trying to move to get a look, Joey grabbed her shoulder, pulling her round he looked into her eyes, she could see the concern but it was the shaking of the head that sent the message.

"They're watching and probably moving even now to get a better firing position" he told her, "We came in that way" he pointed to the top of the rocks where she was going to poke her head over, "the last thing you do is go back that way, they'll be just waiting for that, come on." He half rose and started moving along the natural trench that the rocks had made, sniffer was with them, right at Joey's heel and following obediently.

As soon as they were round a bend in the 'trench' Joey stopped and took out a reel of trip-wire, he took a small rectangular rock and tied one end of the trip wire around it; next he placed the rock on one side of the trench wall, using some other rocks he secured it.

Next he got the duct tape and a grenade out, using the duct tape he taped the grenade securely to the other side of the trench, passing the wire through the eye of the grenade's pin he pulled the wire taught enough that it was hard to see yet not too hard that it popped the pin, then tied it off. Then he took a couple of rocks and hid the whole thing from the side he thought they'd approach from.

"Joey" Sandy sounded urgent; "They're getting closer, sounds like they've found the trench, Get a bloody move on!!" she was almost screaming.

"All finished" he said, 'Now draw their attention," he said and started moving back, he turned back to her and said "Stay here when I get back be ready to run like hell!" and with that, he was gone, back the way they came.

She didn't have to wait long, about fifteen seconds after he disappeared there was a burst of gunfire, she could tell it was the colt, then there was an almighty explosion and Joey reappeared about three seconds later running at full sprint. "Run, NOW!" was all he shouted, she didn't need encouragement and set off at full sprint.

Joey caught up with her just as they heard the next explosion; neither of them fell so that was a good sign wasn't it? They kept running for about a hundred yards, then he indicated for them to slow down, there was no fire from behind so that was a good sign!

"How many?" was all she could think to ask? "How many were there?"

"Don't know for sure" Joey replied, "but I did see five of them, took one down with the gunfire, the others gave chase"

"How many you think there are?"

"Lot more than that!" was all he said, "but we got to keep moving, we're about seven miles from the border.

Just then their worst nightmare became a reality as the heard the whine of huge gas turbine engines, that meant air cover had arrived and it wasn't theirs!

They were at the edge of the rocky outcrop, before them was about a hundred yards of open ground and then a slight dip as the ground began the descent to the river seven miles away, there were trees at the start of the dip that would break their outline up, but cover from the Hind! Nah, he'd see them in seconds especially if they were using night vision.

They took the time to pull their night vision visors down and switch them on, the whole world turned a pale shade of green, but at least they could see where they were going, sniffer was out in front and gave an indication that no one was around, at least he wasn't picking up a scent, that meant they were out of the 'kill zone' and maybe stood a chance of getting out alive.

Gregorovitch couldn't believe his ears, somehow the whole lot had gone 'pear shaped' and instead of having two dead terrorists to deal with he now had a running battle going on and no 'sodding clue' where they were!

"Hinds one and two start immediate pattern patrols" he ordered over his handheld radio, "ten miles north to south along the river, remaining teams close in on the last known location, and be careful!" he was with the main party that was meant to carry out the ambush, they were just behind the party that had fired on Joey, and to be honest if they hadn't been killed in the firefight, he'd have shot them himself, he was that angry with them.

Konrad came on the radio, "Boss, they seem to have headed west, one of the Hinds thinks he just saw them about two miles northwest of your position." He looked at the map just as Konrad said, "I'm sending the other Hind to your position now"

"Roger that, have the Hind slow them down" was all he could say, there was still a sliver of hope they could stop them, if the Hind had them in their sights then it wasn't likely they were going anywhere!

The Hind banked steeply and came round for another pass. They both got as far into the rocks as it was humanly possible, "Think they've seen us?" Sandy asked as the helicopter seemed to pass overhead without using his guns.

"Seems a bit strange that he came round and didn't open up with those canons" Joey replied, "Maybe we got away with it" just as they were about to rise they saw the reason why the Hind had come into a hover and a bunch of men were jumping out the back of the aircraft. "Oh Shit, this gets bloody worse!" Joey whispered a short prayer, 'Any chance you can let up" he looked towards the sky, he wasn't big on praying, but there were times when even the atheist offers one to whatever might be there, this was one of those times!

Eight men, fully armed and ready for war jumped out and started running towards them, this was not going to end well, the other Hind came round and headed straight for them, there was nowhere to hide! It knew exactly where they were and the 30mm canon opened up.

Shells were hitting the earth at six-inch intervals, they started about sixty yards in front of them, and both reacted instantly diving for the nearest cover just as the wave of lead passed over their position.

Sandy went down hard, hitting her head on something, she was groggy and Joey was worried when he saw her, "You okay?" There was no time for a reply; the Hind had come in at 90 degrees to the main force that was about fifteen feet away now. He sat up and instinct took over as he pumped out two grenades from the launcher, the explosions took down three of the group, but these guys knew what they were doing and they were too far apart to take them all down.

Sandy was coherent enough to realize the danger and brought up the AK, she let off a burst at two more, one of the group had almost made the trench when Sniffer launched himself right at the man's throat, the soldier stood no chance as the dog literally ripped his throat out, he just lay there gagging and slowly dying, there was nothing anyone could do, sniffer came straight back into the trench and managed to make it to safety to both their amazement, "And you wanted to get rid of him!" Joey shouted at Sandy.

"Not a bloody chance!" Sandy was vehement, that was the second time the dog had saved them.

"You OK?" Joey asked again, the attackers had retreated to re-group, more were arriving. "I saw you take a nasty bang to the head"

"Just hit the rocks a bit hard" Sandy replied, "I'll be fine" they were both looking for a way out,

Darkness had fallen, but everyone was using night vision gear so that made very little difference, then Sandy saw the way forward. "Joey" she pointed to a slight depression in the ground about two hundred yards north of where they were, "if we can get to there, where we might be able to get around them, what do you think?"

Joey'd been busy reloading the grenade launcher, he took a look and indicated for Sandy to check her ammunition, she had a couple of rounds left in that magazine so she swapped magazines and started clipping loose rounds into the empty one while he thought about the situation, she didn't have to wait long, "Yep, looks like the Russians are waiting for something, they're not looking our way so let's go." Silently they slid out of the trench and made their way crawling on their bellies towards the depression, they were halfway there when an alert Russian cottoned on to what they were doing, even Sniffer had been moving quietly as if he knew the danger they were in.

The Russian was actually waiting for them in the depression, what he wasn't waiting for was sixty pounds of pissed off German Shepherd wanting to rip his throat out, before Joey could even realise what was happening Sniffer had seen the Russian move and launched himself at the prone figure, there was a blood-curdling scream as the dog made contact and a wolf-like growl as teeth and throat met, the man reached for a knife, but Joey got there first and pinned the arm to the ground as Sniffer did his work, Joey was merciful this time and taking the Browning out from its holster he finished the man off quickly, but sniffer just stood there growling over the dead body. Joey really wondered just what was going on in the dog's brain, that was twice he'd ripped the throats out of the Russians!

Alerted by the sounds all hell broke loose again, but this time they were in the depression and running hard again, each step closing in on safety.

There was a clump of trees ahead, they dived for cover behind the trees, rolled and came up firing as the Russians broke cover, another two went down, but there were so many and they were closing in, "Keep running" Joey screamed as he turned and left off another short burst, "they were both on their feet again and heading deeper into the trees.

The 'clump' turned into a small wood, with oak, pine and various other kinds mixed in, Joey slowed them down to almost a snail's pace, the going was slow but the advantage was they weren't making much noise, the enemy had little idea exactly where they were and they were able to move slowly through the wood.

'Crack' they froze, Sniffer's coat was standing on end, his 'hackles' up, a low growl coming out, the noise they'd heard that had seemed to deafen them was just a twig breaking, but it had broken under a human foot, and it wasn't one of theirs, that meant their pursuers were close, close enough to need to be a damn sight more careful than they were being, Sandy indicated it'd come from the left to their south, and it wasn't far away.

Both had full magazines, both could see the river about half a mile away, so near, yet so far. "Only one thing for it" Joey whispered into the mike, Sandy was amazed it was still working, "When I say run for the border and don't stop for anything"

"What?" Sandy stopped and looked at Joey; she didn't like what she was hearing.

"I'll be right behind you" he reassured her, somehow it didn't sound that way.

"No" she was emphatic in her reply, "If we go then we go together!"

"Sandy" Joey spoke softly, "I'll be right behind you"

"After you've done the 'John Wayne' and taken out the bad guys right?" she asked pointedly, "It's crazy, you've no flaming idea how many there are, and you want to flaming well bayonet charge them or something?" She stopped for a moment, cocked the AK and said, "If we do it we do it together! And don't bloody argue!"

"Okay, but as soon as we're through we run like shit for the border! Deal?" he held out his hand.

She took his hand but instead of shaking it she said "deal" then reached in and kissed him full on the lips, "that's for luck" she said.

"I think there's five or six of them," Joey whispered, "we can't take 'em all, the idea is just to rattle them so we can get as far as possible before they open up" he shifted slightly, "as soon as you hear 'em firing start weaving and running in a zig-zag, but not predictable, got that?"

"Yep"

"I expect the Hind will show up when that starts happening. When it does you keep going, I'll deal with it"

"With what?" she was about to ask, then she thought better of it, "I don't want to know how!" was what came out.

Another crack told them the pursuers were getting closer, possibly only a few feet away, Joey gave Sniffer's leash to Sandy, he'd recovered it when sniff attacked the last one, "Ready to get out of here boy?" he spoke to the dog, "You keep Sandy safe for me will you?"

The leash was a good long one, but for this Sandy would need to hold him on a short rein as they couldn't afford for him to get hit by s stray bullet of theirs, she adjusted everything and nodded to Joey, they were ready.

They waited for the pursuers to show themselves, they didn't have to wait long, one of them came out from behind a tree about ten feet away, he was met with a hail of bullets in a scything motion as they both sprang forward screaming at the top of their lungs, both of them emptied their magazines and reloaded before they reached the main group, then they ran as fast as they could.

The Hind was making another searching pass as they broke cover and ran for the border less than a few hundred yards away, Gregorovitch was screaming at the pilot to "Turn this heap of shit round" as the pilot banked hard, he didn't see the two shadows low on the horizon following the river and closing fast, but they'd seen him.

"Hawkeye, this is Hood" the radio burst to life, Simpson pressed the mike, "Go ahead hood"

"Hood, we have the Hind on visual, looks like he's busy searching, possibly engaging your friends"

"Roger Hood, are you in range yet?"

"Hood negative for the Hellfires, but the sidewinders are a different story, we're still about seven miles away"

"Shit" it was Jacko that spoke, "They're still what, five miles out? This'll all be over by the time they get there!" he was highly frustrated.

Joey didn't have time to think about what he was doing, the Hind was making another pass, Sandy had almost made it to the river, he had to buy her those extra few seconds no matter what happened to himself, he dropped to a kneeling position and flicked the weapon to 'grenade launcher' he had no idea whether what he was trying was going to work, but hell, he had to try something.

The Hind helicopter is five tons of flying armour almost all of which is forward and downward facing, even the most advanced anti-armour weaponry just bounces off the armour, but there is one weak point. It just takes a hell of a lucky shot to get it with a grenade launcher that doesn't have a very good sight.

The Hind also carries eight fully armed soldiers in a rear bay, when the door is down they deploy out the back, when they're out the door takes a minute to raise, Joey saw that the door hadn't properly closed as it passed overhead, he broke cover to draw the helicopter off.

Sandy saw him run and almost stopped herself' he was heading away from her, what the hell was he doing?

Just then the helicopter passed overhead and 'opened up' the 30mm canon ripping ground up every few inches.

Joey dived behind a rock just as the rounds got level with him, rolling and coming up he let fly with the grenade launcher, the first two bounced off the door of the helicopter, but the third found a crack between the door and the helicopter.

It went in, passing the door housing, past the armour plating and on into the pilot's cockpit, found a solid surface in the instrument panel where it finally exploded engulfing the whole of the cockpit in a white-hot heat, Joey saw the flames burst out of the cockpit windows just half a second before the fuel in the tanks burst into flames and a fireball thirty feet across sent bits of helicopter flying in all directions, part of the shrapnel came hurtling his way, he just managed to dive for cover as the main part of the helicopter came crashing down.

Sandy heard the explosion and stopped dead, she turned just in time to see Joey swaying and fall, "Joey NOOO!!!" she screamed as she turned and ran back, she skidded to a halt literally scooping his head up, he was barely conscious and in a bad way, "Don't you sodding well dare die on me you arsehole" she screamed, tears rolling down her cheeks, she would have hated him for it if she'd had time to think, but everything was just going crazy.

"Guns are ready boss" Jenny's crewman spoke. "You or me?"

"Thanks, Jimmy" Jenny replied, "you fly the plane I'll deal with the targets" she flicked a switch and her helmet display came to life, from now on everywhere she looked the Gatling canon would follow, all she'd have to do is press the button on the joystick. "Sidewinders are live, I have missile lock" she was speaking over the radio, then she saw the explosion, "Hawkeye this is Hood, the

Hind just got taken down, and it wasn't us, repeat it wasn't us!"

Jimmy took the chopper down and increased the speed, the other chopper was following on their right, they saw the encounter with the Hind and were stunned when the Hind exploded, "Remind me never to argue with that guy!" Jenny said referring to Joey, she saw the soldiers on the ground still planning to press home the attack now he was down, she opened up on them with the Gatling, it was a one-sided competition, the other chopper saw the other Hind and decided to send a message, they opened up with the Gatling canon, bullets ricocheting off the armour plating.

The other Hind got the message, two Longbows against one Hind were not good odds, so he turned tail and got the hell out of there!

"Hawkeye, this is Hood, you're clear to land" she called out as the Lynx came into view. They went straight to where the two were.

The Lynx didn't have time to land before Jacko and Mac were out of the chopper, Mac took one look at the situation and threw open his medical bag, he began treating the wounds immediately, they looked pretty serious, but there was no way he was saying that.

"I don't know Joey" he started, "A bit of a scratch and you've got the girls falling over you!" he started binding the wounds up using a couple of field dressings.

All Joey remembered was Sandy's tears as he faded, he began a thought that it was nice to see before oblivion came knocking.

Chapter 23

The Lynx came in low and fast, the pilot could see the Longbows, one was giving chase to the Hind, not engaging but making sure it stayed well away, the second was banking at the edge of the flat ground, ready to come back.

Small arms fire was coming from the right. "Gunner in the left, medic ready on the right" she ordered.

Smithy had the GPMG (General purpose machine gun, known by soldiers as the Gimpee) and mounted it in a stand, clipping it to the floor he fed the ammo belt in and slammed the housing down, cocking the lever, "ready" he shouted.

"Stand by" the pilot brought the chopper over the two figures, they could see one was down but had no idea who.

The gun blasted the rocks where the fire had been coming from. Splinters flying everywhere, the Longbow had made its turn and was coming back to join in giving the suppression fire. The occasional shot was still coming from the rocks, but mostly the Russians were keeping their heads down or trying to get out of there.

Jacko and Mac didn't wait for them to land, as soon as they saw them underneath they jumped, Jacko almost landed on Sandy and took up a defensive kneel watching for any movement. Mac threw her aside "out the way lassie" he tried to be gentle but there was a bit too much urgency, "Let me work" his hands moved with lightning speed, finding out where Joey's wounds were and which was most important.

"Shrapnel in both the shoulder and abdomen" Mac began, "they're the worst, the head wound's just a nasty knock" Joey had a nasty gash above his right eye. "He'll need surgery and a blood transfusion." He looked up, "corporal, wheres those bloody field dressings I told you to get me?" two field dressings came flying out of the body of the Lynx, the crewman, a corporal also climbed out of the helicopter.

"Can we move him?"

"As soon as I've got these field dressings on" Mac didn't even look up, he was busy unpacking the larger field dressing, he took the outer packaging and making sure it was still clean he applied the outer package to wound in his abdomen with the inside directly touching the skin, that way the sterile waterproof side stayed sterile, then as soon as that was on he took the bandage and began binding the dressing to the wound, there was shrapnel in the wound that he was careful around but he left it in the wound as that was a problem for the doctors at the nearest hospital, not for the Battlefield!

He kept the dressing tight so that would keep the pressure on the wound and restrict the blood flow from the wound, he didn't want to cut blood flow off totally, just restrict it so that there wasn't a lot of flow, stemming it totally was a problem for the doctors too. Next, he did the same to the shoulder, as soon as that was done he signalled the colonel and Sandy, "Let's get him in the chopper" he shouted above the noise of the engines, "and get the hell out of here"

Smithy was still manning the machine gun, but resistance was almost non-existent now and they'd stopped firing, instead the Russians could be seen trying to retreat and get out of the line of fire, he'd stopped firing but was keeping a wary eye on them, the second Longbow was also back with them and both attack helicopters were doing the same.

"Let's get the hell out of here" It was Jacko ordered the pilots, "Where's the nearest hospital?"

"There's a medical station on the base at Kirkuk" the pilot replied, "about a twenty minute flight"

They were just loading the unconscious Joey as a black shadow darted towards them; Jacko instinctively swivelled and raised the rifle.

"No" Sandy screamed as she lunged knocking the rifle just as Jacko pulled the trigger, the round went harmlessly wide, "The dog's with us" she shouted above the noise, an angry defiant look on her face that took on a sinister glow.

"What the hell?" Jacko didn't get chance to finish before she cut in again.

"That dog saved our lives twice in the last couple of hours!" She nodded in Sniffers direction. "So he comes with us, AND DON'T BLOODY ARGUE!" she calmed down a little, "His name's Sniffer, he's one of the dogs they were using to track us, the rest I'll explain at the debriefing, but it will have to wait"

Sniff had jumped into the chopper and laid next to Joey, somehow he knew Mac was trying to help Joey, so he was letting him near, but he was barking like crazy out the door on the other side, clearly warning the Russians to stay away, not that they were considering anything else. Everyone else climbed in and they were away.

Chapter 24

Sandy was nervous, and annoyed with herself for being so. She couldn't explain it and thought that people would laugh at her for it, but she felt like a teenager with a 'crush' and it annoyed her.

Yet at the same time she was beginning to enjoy the feeling, the feeling that someone had finally penetrated the armour she'd put around herself, she was annoyed that Joey probably had no idea just how much she was thinking of him.

Joey's injuries weren't as serious as they'd looked, Mac had been right about that, it turned out the most serious were the blow to the head and the leg where a piece of shrapnel narrowly missed the femoral artery.

It was the wounding that showed her she actually did care about this boy! He was a couple of years older than her, but there was something 'boyish' about him she hadn't figured out yet.

Joey wasn't much better, he'd liked Sandy from the start, but the last couple of weeks had been pretty intense, he knew it was the real her and not the masquerade he'd seen, but did she like him the same?

"She's way out of my league" had been his thought on more than one occasion, and he couldn't get past the idea that she should be 'dating' some officer and not an 'average soldier' but there was another part of him that said. "Stuff the sodding rules, why can't we be an item?"

He'd just finished packing his stuff when there was a knock at the door, it began to open.

Joey was glad he was sitting down as Sandy entered, his stomach tightened and he was sure if he was standing he'd be weak at the knees seeing her. He struggled to his feet, almost falling over.

"You ready?" She spoke quietly; she had a beautiful soft accent he couldn't quite place.

Sandy was wearing a one-piece sleeveless dress that came to just below the knees. The deep blue of the dress complimenting her deep red hair and giving her skin the appearance of pure alabaster, her sparkling blue eyes shone like diamonds, he opened his mouth to speak but no sound came out, he just nodded, then plucked up the courage. "Sandy" he began, "I need to say" that was as far as he got.

She took a step forward, held up her right index finger and gently pressed it to his lips. "I know what you're going to say?" She was quiet but firm, "here's my reply" and with that she stepped so they were toe to toe, their eyes locked, then she slowly reached out with both hands and took each of his hands in hers.

Gently she moved them so his hands were around her waist, then she let go and gently reached up, taking his face in her cupped hands she placed a long and sensitive kiss, pulling away she looked him in the eye, Joey was in a daze, "I know all the reasons why not" she said, "but I really don't care about them, this is what I want!" She stopped there and waited.

"But Sandy" he began, he didn't recognize his own voice, he was so nervous it was almost a whisper. "What will" was as far as he got.

"In case you forgot" Sandy interrupted, "You're not in the Army at the moment! So that 'fraternizing' rule can't apply can it?" She looked into his eyes; she could see his confusion dissolving into the mist. "Besides we'll never have secrets between us, will we?"

"We'll never need to" he replied, then stepping closer, his hands moved so he was no longer holding her but gently caressing, their faces almost touching he spoke softly, "then here's my reply" and he gently kissed her, a long lingering kiss that grew in intensity with every heartbeat.

If you enjoyed this book, then please take a look
The next few pages are a glimpse of the next
book in the series.
'Scorpion's Reach'

Chapter 1

The tide had turned, but the wind hadn't. It was picking up, causing the waves to grow as they came in on the beach. The two vehicles raced across the sand to the meeting point. The sea wasn't too rough, but it was choppy, and not a night to be out.

"They should be coming in over there," the man in the passenger seat of the lead vehicle, a black Ford Ranger spoke. They were here to meet someone, or something, being brought in by helicopter; they had no idea who they were meeting, apart from 'They must be important'. The passenger pointed to a slight outcrop. "We need to set the HLS up over there, by the flat piece of beach" he pointed to where the beach was at its widest.

"Bloody idiots must be nuts trying to land in this damn wind" the driver, a big man probably in his late thirties with dark leathery skin and a beer paunch replied, "I mean, it must be a bloody cross wind of thirty miles an hour. What the hell's the rush?" he hated these kinds of jobs. Just "Be there at this time and keep your trap shut" kind of thing, "And don't ask what you're unloading" etc was the rule and a damn good idea to stick to it, which stifled the next question he had.

"I know what you're thinking" the passenger a slightly older man in his early forties with lighter skin and a scar on the left cheek just below the ear. "Don't go there, and I've no idea anyway!" he scanned the skies for signs of the aircraft they were supposed to be meeting. "Not here yet, pull over and kill the lights" they did so, the vehicle behind did the same.

As soon as they stopped and the lights were off the man in the vehicle behind got out, took a moment, moved forward lighting a cigarette and sauntered forward like he hadn't a care in the world, in reality he was scanning everything, making sure no one was watching, he stopped at the driver's side, then pulled two other cigarettes out and offered them one each.

"These things will kill you!" Sam, the driver spoke as he took the cigarette and lit it, they all smiled.

"At least these will take a while to do that" he replied, "This job can do it in seconds, and without bloody warning." They all gave a small chuckle. "Any ideas what this is about?" he stopped for a moment; knowing he shouldn't really be asking, but it wasn't as if they were going to tell the bosses: they'd all be in the shit if anyone did.

"Not a sodding clue bro," the passenger who went by the name of big Jake replied. He was their leader, "The last shipment was only a couple of days ago, so I doubt it's a shipment; unless the dumbass trendy set in Auckland have been buying up large" that brought a chuckle from the others, but he carried on scanning the horizon, "But must be important if they want it, or them, delivered this quick!"

"Come on, let's get these damn things out and set up so they come into the wind" the older man spoke to the other two as they headed round to the back of the first Ranger, he unlocked and opened the back hatch, they had five lights for the Tee and another special one that would guide the aircraft down, all ex military surplus, designed to give an instant landing pad for a helicopter but with the advantage that unless the 'aircraft' came in on the exact bearing the lights couldn't be seen, and the other advantage of using these was that the one coming in wouldn't need any landing lights.

They set the lights out in the form of a 'T', with the long part running east to west along the beach, each light about three meters apart. Only small perforations on one side where the light would shine through, unless you were almost directly in front of them there's no way you could see the lights, they were designed for landing a helicopter when you don't want people to know you're coming, or don't want people like the local authorities to find you, not so good if you're looking for the hele landing site without knowing what bearing you need to approach on. That's why the bearing and information were so important.

Next, Big Jake, took another box that looked like it had a torch welded to the top and flicked the switch, that one would give the pilot his/her height as they came in, a simple red, yellow and green system. If the light was red the pilot was too low, if it was yellow they were too high, but in the middle was the green that as the pilot stayed in the green by the time they got close to the light they'd see the beach coming up to meet them and be literally about four feet from them right at the end, and all without landing lights!

"All set?" Jake looked up and spoke just loud enough to be heard by the others who were heading back to the vehicles.

"Yep, all done" the one who'd driven the second vehicle, a younger guy with gang tattoos on his right cheek spoke up, "Just getting my stuff from the Ranger"

"Okay, I'll send the text" Jake spoke up again. He took a small mobile phone out of his pocket, one tap and the screen came alive, two more taps and he was putting the phone away, the message sent. "Now we wait" was all he said after that.

The 'text' was a simple set of letters and numbers. The receiver was wired into the pilot's console in the aircraft; a Bell Jetranger that right at that moment was approaching the coast further up North East.

The pilot was flying by instinct with all his external lights off and the lights in the cockpit dimmed as much as he could get away with to minimize the effect it had on his eyesight, the more light in the cab the less he'd see outside. He also knew he was only about fifty feet above the top of the waves (one hundred feet above sea level), one slight twitch, and they'd been 'in the drink' and sinking so fast that even a life jacket was useless, they'd be pulled under still clipped into the chopper and blades still spinning above them, ready to chop everything and everyone in half who tried to 'bale out' choppers aren't that good for 'ditching' like that.

He could see the coast ahead and was heading for the beach when he heard a beeping, it was the message coming through.

"Message for you" a voice spoke into his headset, it was the computer in the phone he'd wired into the system, one of the latest Iphones with a few little extras added.

"Read" he spoke back to the phone, the passenger he was carrying gave him a quizzical look, then, realizing that he wasn't actually talking to him turned and carried on ignoring him, he was just the 'delivery boy' after all.

"Charlie, Bravo, two four zero, ten, one hundred" the voice, a female voice devoid of all feeling came back, it was meant to be functional, but also not the kind of voice you'd expect in a machine so that it forced you to pay attention to what it was saying.

He understood the message perfectly, it was his directions to the landing site telling him "At the coast turn bearing two forty degrees for ten miles, stay at a height of one hundred feet" he knew that using the lights they were using for landing he'd see the red 'guide light' first telling him he was too low, he'd see that from about five miles away but keep going and the others would come into sight.

Eventually the light will turn green, and that's when to begin the descent, the rest was simple. Just slow down and stay in the green and the lights will do the rest; he'll feel the skids touch the sand and that's the time say goodbye to the passenger, that wouldn't be too hard as this passenger hadn't been the most talkative he'd had.

"If you're in the red, you'll soon be dead" he mumbled to himself, 'What's the rest of the saying? Yellow so high you need a Halo, Green you'll be seen and come in mean! Something like that anyway' he finished the thought off in his head.

"Any ideas when this clown's supposed to show?" Sam asked for the second time that night, they'd gone through two cigarettes each and were fast running out of smokes because 'as usual' he was the only one who brought any, and as soon as the work was done they all wanted one.

"Told you" Jake replied, "No idea bro, and don't ask questions, they can get you seriously hurt with these people!"

"So?" Sam stubbed his cigarette out in the ashtray in the back door, "when are these clowns going to show up do you think?"

"Everyone's a clown to you" Henry, the other one in the trio shot back, "you've got to be careful saying things like that" he stubbed his cigarette out too, "saying it to the wrong person could get you kissing the barrel of a 9 millimetre!"

"And who'd they get to do this crap with you lot?" Sam replied laughing. "Some other poor sod fresh out of stir and no prospects for any meaningful employment!"

That was the 'top and bottom of it. One stupid mistake as a teenager and no one wants to help out. Been to prison? Forget a decent job or income, they just aren't going to come your way and that's a fact, the only ones want to know you are the ones who got you into trouble in the first place,

"Anyway, less of the bitching about life's choices and let's get this job done, looks like the chopper's about to arrive!" Henry spoke as he opened the Ranger's door and got ready to climb in, they could hear the faint but constant whine of a Gas turbine engine along with the constant but distant 'thwack' that the rotors made as the two blades sliced through the air violently pushing the air out of the way.

"Come on boys" Henry spoke loudly as he finished climbing into of the vehicle, "Let's get this over with, then we can all go home and 'lament' the lack of good jobs for us as those pricks head off to their offices and dead end jobs and we count the grand that we got for being here and doing 'sweet Fanny Adams' if you know what I mean!"

"True" Big Jake chuckled, "Does kind of beat working doesn't it?"

"Yeah" Sam joined, "Just don't ask stupid questions, or you might find yourself with an extra ventilation hole or two, know what I mean!"

"Oh I dunno" Henry chipped in, "I love work, I can watch people doing it all day long" that brought a few more chuckles from the others.

"What's it sodding well matter as long as they pay well?" Jake was laughing, but getting a little impatient..

"Okay" Sam came back, "I'll drop it, for now." They all knew that they were going to have the same conversation all over again the next time they got to do a pick up.

The helicopter was about a hundred yards away when Jake spoke up. "Time for us to make ourselves scarce" he reached down and pressed the starter, she started first time. The instructions had been very clear, wait until the 'chopper' is inbound then leave and don't look back, you'll be told in a few days where to pick the vehicle and lights up."

He put the Ranger into gear and began to pull away as the helicopter began its final approach, whatever or more like whoever was arriving, the bosses, whoever they were didn't want anyone to know about, that was fine as the three of them had no intention of thinking about finding out.

"The ground party are on their way" the passenger spoke with a slight Eastern European accent, his voice devoid of all emotion, he sounded more mechanical than Human. "You can land now" it felt like an order, and Carlos wasn't too good at taking orders normally, this time was different though.

As soon as the passenger got in the aircraft the temperature in it dropped, it was as if death itself was riding with him, and he just wanted this guy gone, so if that meant keeping his mouth shut until the job was done then that's what he'd do. He got the impression that guy wasn't into talking that much anyway.

The whole forty five minutes of the flight they were the first words he'd spoken, not even a greeting at the beginning, even the drug mules taking the shipments ashore, as hyped as they usually were still at least gave a greeting; as if to steady their nerves. They never really knew what was waiting for them at the other end, but this guy was a whole different kettle of fish.

It wasn't that he was wary, or at least didn't seem that way, to him it just seemed as if he was going to a regular job, he just gave the impression that to ask what that job was, might be more than your life was worth. Carlos was glad he was getting rid of the 'package' and good riddance.

The Helicopter's skids touched the sand, the passenger hit the release button on his five point harness, he opened the door, with his left hand and climbed out, closing the door, he opened the back and took out a heavy suitcase. As soon as he had the case he closed the door and without even looking to the pilot to get the 'OK' he just headed out forwards from under the rotor blades.

As soon as he was clear he headed for the Ranger and opened the driver's door looking for the electronic key that would open the back of the Ranger.

"Arrogant prick" Carlos thought to himself as he lifted back off the ground, "Not even acknowledging the ride!" He was angry, but knew there was no point making any noise about it. They paid well and didn't give a shit what you thought of them. Just as long as he delivered the good when they told him to.

And money was what he needed. A struggling business and a willingness to, do anything that helps pay the bills was what got him the job, at first it seemed like a good job to have, ferrying a few things around so the cops didn't know where they were, a few plants and stuff, then it got slowly more serious until they had him 'by the balls,' and he was carting the hard stuff for them. Always at a moment's notice. He'd get a call and would have to drop anything that was planned to get the job done, asking questions wasn't an option.

As soon as Carlos was airborne he turned on a fresh bearing that would take him out to sea, ten minutes would see him fifteen miles off shore, then he'd be able to climb to five hundred feet and come back onto radar for the little charade that fitted with his flight plan.

On the beach the lone passenger watched the Helicopter depart, he was glad to be alone and not having to deal with the stupid vermin that he often had to deal with in his profession, these people weren't particularly any worse than the others, they all annoyed him, but the pay was good and as soon as he'd got this job done he could disappear, until they needed his special skills again. Back to his own little world where he was left in peace and the rest of the world didn't intrude.

As soon as he got to the vehicle he went to the driver's door and opened it, the keyless ignition and door sensor were on the seat; he reached in and scooped them up. Pressing the button for the rear door he heard the click as the door opened. He put the suitcase on the rear seat but still opened the rear hatch, the pickup, or 'Ute' as they called them here, had a covered back tray.

As soon as the helicopter was gone he walked round to each of the lights in turn, turned them off and picked them up, carrying them to the ute (Short for 'utility vehicle') he put them in the back in the special container they'd come from, he didn't bother to wipe the sand off them or to wipe them down from the moisture, the 'minions' could do that when they got them back in a few days.

Five minutes later everything was packed up and he was ready to roll, he climbed into the driver's seat and reaching inside his coat he took a plain manila envelope out,

The envelope had nothing written on the outside, but he knew from previous experience that all the details he would need were in the envelope including the passport he'd be using to leave the country and the route they'll want him to take after the job was done, but most importantly for this stage there were the details of the passwords to access the encrypted files he'd already got on his laptop in his suitcase, all he knew was the target was in Auckland and he had a seven hour drive ahead.

He pressed the starter, she started up first time, putting the vehicle into gear he set off, there was no need to worry about tyre tracks as the sea was almost up to the vehicle by now, within the hour the sea would cover the landing site and all trace of tonight's meeting would be lost.

Chapter 2

The scenery took his breath away, rather it took most of it, and what the scenery didn't take the ride did.

Joey still wasn't fully one hundred percent fit after Iran, the wounds had left him in hospital unable to do much for nearly a month, then the Doc had told him "No exercise for at least another month" and Sandy had insisted on making sure that he obeyed fully, she'd taken it on herself to make sure he 'did it' right, she'd become his own 'personal nurse.'

Not that he was complaining, he was actually over the moon about it, but he'd never even dream of letting on.

"Come on slow coach" Sandy turned and shouted over her right shoulder as she approached the next bend in the road, the hills weren't big, but they were constant, and besides the scenery to the left was the kind that if you caught a glimpse, it would stop you dead in your tracks as you tried to take it in, Joey wasn't a religious person, but seeing this scenery was almost a 'spiritual experience'

The mountains weren't tall enough to be snow capped, but the rocky peaks surrounded by emerald green forests that hadn't been touched by man, and cascaded down the slopes until they suddenly dropped onto beaches, not 'pristine white' beaches but messy untouched and littered with driftwood, the things that the sea herself deposits on beaches, the kind of things that say "Man's not been here. And he better not touch me."

For Joey, coming from a place that's teeming with people and you can't see the beaches for deck chairs and stuff, seeing such untouched beauty was stunning, he hadn't really believed that such places still existed, but here they were, and they were everywhere on this Island.

The beaches themselves were sided by steep cliffs on one side and a turquoise sea that in places actually bubbled as the earth's crust was so thin that it warmed the water in places, at one point the other day they'd actually taken a hot bath in seawater on the beach!

There were four of them altogether; Joey and Sandy along with Sandy's sister Helen and her husband Kevin, a 'good kiwi bloke' as he loved to say. Straight after the hospital Joey and the team had a meeting with Sir Michael who basically said, "You're too valuable to go back to your old regiment so we're transferring you to M.I.6 as soon as Joey's well enough to carry on."

That was it, Joey's days in the Army were over, the days as "Bond, James Bond" as he tried to say in a pathetic Scottish accent were just beginning.

"First order of the day" Sir Michael had continued, "Phoenix is wounded, but they're not finished, they want blood. AND WE MEAN YOURS" he'd looked around the room at the team. "Apparently they want your heads served up on a silver platter and preferably severed from your bodies, they're willing to pay a high price for them!"

"That along with the unholy political row that Iran caused" he went on. "Means we need you folks out of the way for a while" he shifted in his seat as he said the words, the rest of the team just looked at each other not sure whether they were liking what they heard, moving to M.I.6 was a huge pay increase and they'd get to play with a lot more 'cool gadgets' but the Army was all most of the team had ever wanted, taking it away like this seemed a bit cruel.

"Jacko" Sir Michael continued, "You and Mac are going to Canberra, the Aussie SAS would like to learn a few things from you, officially still with the Regiment, but at my beck and call" he didn't even pause as he turned to Smithy, "You're going to Burnham down in New Zealand, the Defence force there want a sniper instructor"

"What about us sir?" Joey'd stopped him in his tracks and was somewhat impatient.

"We're going on Holiday" it was Sandy that replied, "Don't argue!" she looked Joey in the eye, she knew he'd want to get back into the thick of things. "You need to recover some more, and besides I haven't said where yet, New Zealand, to see my sister and her husband"

"Oh" was all he could say, not sure how to take the 'meet the family' routine.

"You'll love it," Sandy replied. "They're the real outdoors people, just the kind you love"

The road that runs around the coast of New Zealand is known as the Pacific Highway. In places, near the big cities it's a wide open road, sometimes with dual carriageways, at other times, near the smaller places it's just a single carriageway round the Island, and in some of the more remote places, it isn't even a mettled road, just a gravel road; often clinging to the cliffs with sheer drops into the ocean.

Just north of Thames, on the Coromandel peninsular it's a single carriageway, but go too far and she gives way to gravel road. They were still on the single carriageway, just south of Coromandel township, a small settlement near the northern end of the peninsular, a winding road at the best of times.

The rest of them were up at the hairpin bend, admiring the view, Joey wasn't that far behind, and besides, he could have easily kept up with them, but Sandy had explained that part of the job was not telling folks what you did, and being 'too fit' after a serious accident (that was the story) would kind of give the game away a little, it would have people a bit too suspicious, so he'd played along with it and was taking his time, but being called a 'slowcoach' was pushing it even if it was his beloved saying it.

The other three were on the small grass verge as he got to the bend, Kevin a born naturalist and ardent conservationist was explaining something to the two girls,

Joey couldn't quite hear what he was saying but he followed their gaze to the creatures frolicking in the bay, there were a group of large black and white creatures swimming and diving in the water between the islands in the bay, the closest of them was probably only about two hundred yards off the shore.

"Are they?" Joey began, and then it dawned on him what they were watching. "That's a pod of Orcas!" was more a statement than a question, the only time Joey'd ever seen Orcas was on TV. "I thought they lived in the Arctic?"

"They do in the Arctic summer" Kevin replied. "And in southern Ocean in the Southern Summer, the Hauraki Gulf is a stopping off point on their journey, kind of a whale's refuelling station, they're stopping off for a feed in the bay"

They were mesmerized, watching a pod of creatures as majestic as the Orca is something special, even in New Zealand you could spend hundreds of dollars paying to go out beyond the horizon 'whale watching' and still not see a sight as amazing as twenty to thirty Orcas just feeding in the bay, what made it even more special was that just a little further away was another pod, but this one was Dolphins, and the two didn't seem to be bothering each other.

"Do the Orcas feed on Dolphins?" It was Helen asked the question that all wanted to know.

"Sometimes" Kevin replied, "But these seem to not be bothering with the Dolphins as they tend to fight back as a group"

"Kind of a don't screw with us then?" Joey asked cheekily. He was fascinated that the Dolphins would band together and protect each other.

"Put it this way" Kevin replied, "If they did feed on Dolphins, they wouldn't be welcome here! The Dolphins keep sharks away and they're probably Hector's dolphins, they're only found in New Zealand waters"

"Yeah" Helen agreed, "Dolphin's hunt Sharks don't they?" she asked.

"Not just that" Kevin continued, "but if anyone's in danger from sharks, the dolphins will come in and attack the shark, often driving it off and saving the people"

That bit was a bit too much, both Joey and Sandy broke out into a disbelieving smile, but neither said anything for fear of offending their hosts, Kevin saw it and jumped back in with 'proof' "I'll show the articles on the net when we get back" he spoke up, "Where people were swimming and the dolphins protected them! By the way, Orcas think sharks are tasty!"

James Cavell was an arrogant prick and not only did he know it, he really didn't give a damn what people thought of him, not even his boss at the Bank!

'When you make people tons of money' he thought to himself often 'They really don't give a toss what you're like' and he was making them bucket loads of cash, so he really didn't give a damn what people thought of him.

He'd been with the Bank just two years and in that time he'd made them a whole bundle of money that is if you didn't look too close at the clients and some of the things they got up to.

But that was 'work' and right now he just couldn't care less about it. The sun was shining, the road was quiet, a gorgeous blonde in the passenger seat.

He knew she too only wanted his money, she wasn't an 'escort' or whatever they called themselves, but only thing she wanted was his dough.

Truth was that was okay, he'd spend a little on her over the weekend, and maybe one two more weekends then it'll be the old 'heave ho' and find another, that's the way he lived his life, and he loved it.

The weekend they'd got planned was a simple 'romantic weekend' away from the city at his place overlooking the bay north of Coromandel Township. The bay was one of the most magical one you could imagine with emerald islands set in turquoise seas where amazing sea life can be seen.

"Snorkelling and sex" was all that was on his mind, and not necessarily in that order, the blonde was 'hot' after all and well, he just might not be able to hold himself back from sampling the delights of what she was offering! The road was the last thing on his mind.

Then again in a McLaren P1 you didn't need to do too much thinking about the road, the car did the thinking for you.

A formula one engine accelerates you from zero to sixty miles an hour or one hundred kilometres an hour in just under three seconds, the speed topping out at just over two hundred miles an hour making it a true 'supercar'

The traction control system keeps the car literally glued to the road as if with superglue, and human control is just too slow so it's all controlled by computer, yet just enough is left to the human that it feels as if the car is under the driver's control making it not just a good drive but a whole new amazing experience for anyone lucky enough to amass so much wealth.

The road from Auckland to Thames had been reasonably busy with the cops patrolling and people keeping their speed down, still it had only taken about two hours for the hundred mile trip, but most of the traffic was turning right just before Thames and heading to Whitianga or Whangamata. 'Where the wannabes go' he thought to himself.

Cavell had a place in a secluded spot right on the beach halfway between Coromandel Township and Colville. A million dollar plus place that, well probably better the bank didn't know about it as they might get worried just what he was doing with the clients money.

The McLaren was cruising along just in second gear at the one hundred kilometers or sixty miles an hour speed limit. Frustration was beginning to show, he just wanted the chance to 'open her up.' That would come just after Thames, followed by hairpins and enjoyable roads as he tore along scaring the life out of anything he would meet on that road.

They pulled up at the last set of lights in Thames right next to a Porsche 911 Cayman, the other driver gave a look that clearly meant "not impressed" and revved the engine, it wasn't even a contest. The Porsche can do standing start to sixty in just over three seconds, the McLaren does it in two and a half!

They stayed behind the Porsche until they got round the first bend, the other driver must have thought he had them beat; but on the long straight stretch Cavell let her loose. The McLaren growled with delight, wheels spinning she blew past the other car as if it was parked, the long face and dropped jaw on the other driver said it all. She was flying. Cavell eased off the accelerator but she kept accelerating faster and faster as if the foot was to the floor, eating up road like a ravenous beast devouring prey; He tried the brake, really sluggish, something wasn't right, they should have responded well. He tried again, even worse. Pumping the brake nothing happened, the brakes failed and the throttle stuck open, not good.

"Not good at all" he was beginning to panic

"James" Denise, the girl with him was looking worried. "Don't you think you should slow down?"

"I'm trying" he wanted to shout, it didn't come out as a shout though, more like a whisper he was concentrating so hard, he grabbed for the handbrake and began pulling, they'd reached a hundred and ten miles an hour and she was still accelerating, a slight right hand bend fast approaching, crashing the car crossed his mind except one side was rock and the other a twenty foot drop, neither were good options

"The accelerator's stuck" was all he could say, he was pumping the pedals as hard as he could, nothing was happening, "and the brakes aren't working"

"What?" she looked across at him worried.

The car was doing over a hundred and twenty miles an hour now and still accelerating hard. There was no way they were going to make the hairpin that was coming up, the only hope they had was for him to try and 'drift' the car round the bend, but with the traction control still engaged the chances of drifting were much reduced, there were people at the bend that he was probably going to hit, there was nothing he could do about it, it was either him or them and he knew whom he'd choose. The bend was fast approaching. He swung the steering wheel hard to the right to try and make the bend, still pumping the brakes to try and get the last ounces of fluid to apply the brakes just enough to get them round the bend, there was no time to worry about what next.

The car turned and slid sideways, the McLaren was so low on the ground and the centre of balance was so low that there was no way it was going to roll, but centrifugal force did take over and the car instead of going forward was now moving sideways; tyres squealing, rubber burning and inching forward, but every inch forward meant a foot sideways with the crash barrier fast getting closer.

The four people at the bend were trying to dive out of the way as the passenger side of the car slammed into the crash barrier with a force that ripped the crash barrier clean off the support posts like tearing through a paper barrier and kept going; airbags deployed instantly but the force of the impact still threw them violently sideways almost snapping their necks.

Denise bore the full impact of the crash, the door moving back into her body and breaking every rib, two of them puncturing her left lung and a third going straight through her heart, she was killed instantly. Cavell wasn't so lucky; he was still alive when someone found him.

The vehicle came to a stop on its roof at the bottom of the incline. Cavell wasn't sure how long he was 'out for' only that when he came too he was upside down, held firmly in place by the four point harness that was the vehicle seat belt, a proper racing harness similar to those used in racing cars.

There was blood on just about every surface inside the vehicle, He tried to open his eyes, but only one obeyed, a misty red scene awaited him as he tried to look around, searing pain in his lower abdomen told him there was probably some serious internal damage, he could feel his feet, but not move them, he was trapped.

Out of his good eye he could see Denise, she was a mess, blood covering most of her face, and she was clearly dead. As he looked at her he saw another moving round the vehicle, a man wearing all black. He didn't get a clear view as the man seemed to be keeping his face out of sight, what he did see was a very slight build that seemed to move with grace and purpose round the vehicle.

"Help" Cavell tried to shout, but all that came out was a whisper, he looked for his 'Angel' to see what he was doing. He felt strong hands moving round his neck. "Checking my injuries" he thought to himself.

His sense of relief turned to alarm as those hands grasped a firm vice like grip on his neck and gave a violent twist severing his spinal column at the base of the brain. The last thought he would ever have didn't have time to form before oblivion descended forever.

Chapter 3

Joey saw or rather heard the car approaching and something just didn't seem right. It sounded like the engine was screaming, almost like whoever the idiot was driving it, were they trying to blow the engine? Something just didn't sound right. He stopped and looked behind, he saw it didn't look right either, careering round the bends at breakneck speed, then it tried to take the hairpin and drifted.

"Everyone out the way NOW" he screamed, and dived for Sandy to knock her out of the way, he'd felt the air disturbance as the car passed, Sandy was knocked into the crash barriers but he couldn't help that, 'she's gonna be pissed with me' he thought, but there wasn't anything he could do, he had to get her out of harm's way!

They landed hard on the tarmac, he stayed conscious, but hurting from just about every joint in his body, the aftermath of wounds not completely healed, yet being called on again to 'lay it on the line' but not for Queen and country this time. "You okay?" he asked as soon as he saw movement from Sandy, she was stirring and shaking her head.

"Think so" Sandy replied as she came round, "Apart from a whacking great headache, what about you?" she turned and looked over in his direction, he could see she wasn't quite focusing yet, "and what the hell were you doing?"

"Didn't exactly help my healing if that's what you mean" he replied, "But otherwise we just about got out of the way in time"

"What the hell happened?"

"Didn't you see the Sports car behind us?" he asked, "I think it was a McLaren."

"No" Sandy replied, is that what it was?" she asked pointing to where the car had gone through the barrier, they could see it, on it's roof a ways down the bank, wheels still spinning."

"Yeah" Joey replied, "looked like they lost control, but they were going at a hell of a speed, bloody crazy trying to take that bend at that speed!" he'd finished checking himself for injuries and started scanning Sandy, "Anywhere you hurt?" it was important they make sure they weren't injured before they started looking for Helen and Kevin. 'Try moving your toes"

Sandy brought each leg up and set them down again, she also wiggled her toes so they could see them moving in the shoes. "Nah, nothing broken" she replied, "Just going to have one hell of a bruise". She went to turn over and tried to move her left arm, "Shit, that HURT" she almost shouted as she nursed the limp arm.

Joey did a quick examination, "Could be a break, or a dislocation" he said. "Let's get it in a sling" he started looking for something to use.

"Find Helen and Kevin" She ordered, "I'll sort out a sling, but can you go look for them please?" she changed her tone slightly; feeling special that he was paying so much attention to her, but there were others needed help, and she really didn't want to get into the 'ordering her man about' scenario.

"Okay, but first call the Ambulance" Joey reached for the mobile he was carrying in his pocket, he handed it to Sandy, it had some interesting features on the phone, for one thing it was constantly monitored by M.I.6 and they both knew that Sir Michael would know of the accident before they got off the phone, it really was an emergency phone where they could be contacted at all times.

"I, I'm okay". Sandy was a little shaky, Joey wanted to stay with her, but knew what was coming next. "You need to go check the others, see if they're okay, please" she grimaced clearly in pain, but a steely determined look he'd learned to recognize and not argue with came onto her face.

The first rule in accident first aid is 'triage' or in other words, find and treat the most serious patients first, Sandy was injured but nowhere near the most serious injury; the others would be worse.

"Give me the phone and get a move on!" Sandy was taking charge, "I'll call the ambulance" he pulled the phone out, tapped the emergency number and handed it to her as soon as the operator came on the line.

"Which service do you require?"

Joey was already moving when he heard Sandy say "Ambulance" truth was they were going to need all three, but the comms centers for all three were linked, as soon as one got the call, the others would pick it up and prioritize with the fatalities and injuries putting them right up there at the top. He could hear her giving details as he moved away.

The car had taken a ten meter section of the crash barrier with it as it went down the incline. There was a gaping hole right there, and only the empty posts at the end of the section. He could see where the barriers had been ripped from the posts with the force of the car's momentum, he took a quick look down the incline, the sight that met his eyes was gruesome.

Kevin had been next to them, with Helen a little further along, he could see Kevin, at least what was left of him and it was horrible.

Joey'd seen some pretty rough things in his time, but this was 'right up there' with the worst of them. The car had been travelling at speed and had trapped him between the car and the crash barrier literally slicing him almost completely in two. Kevin's torso and legs lay at an angle that even if the spine was broken there's no way they could twist that way and still be connected to the body.

"Guess that answers that one" Joey said quietly to himself. "Better concentrate on finding the living" he began looking again, first scanning the incline to check if she was there.

He found her at the other end of where the crash barrier re-started. She'd been hit a glancing blow and thrown over the barrier, she wasn't breathing.

Normally you'd make sure not to move an injured person as you might do more damage and could end up paralysing them for life, the only exception is when they're not breathing, you have to get them breathing again and that means doing CPR or 'Cardiopulmonary Resuscitation'. Joey got straight into it without even thinking.

First thing he did was check the mouth to make sure there was nothing blocking the airway, a quick visual check and a poke around with his fingers cleared the mouth of the two teeth that had been knocked out.

He was careful, tilting the head back trying really hard not to move her head too far so that he didn't move the spine any more than he absolutely had to then he pinched the nose and took a deep breath, then leaning over 'mouth to mouth' he breathed into her mouth.

"Six breaths and massage the heart" was his thought as he lay the head down and moved to the chest, one hand above the other he pushed hard and reasonably fast on her sternum, six hard quick pushes and he was back to the breaths. He kept going alternating between the two until he heard the sound of sirens.

Joey's senses were in overdrive. He was working giving Helen the CPR but at the same time his brain was taking everything in and noting where everything was, the threat assessment part of his training had kicked in big time.

There were no immediate threats to him and Sandy but it was the little things his brain was noticing as he worked on Helen, noticing yet not actively looking. Noticing tyre tracks down on the beach, they were new and looked like 4x4 tracks, then a man seemingly clad in black walking away from the McLaren. Joey wanted to yell to the guy but something stopped him, he didn't think much of it at the time and he had enough to do so he just 'filed the information' to talk to the cops about when they took his statement.

"I'll take over now sir" he half looked up as a fireman threw himself down beside him and motioned him to move over, he gladly gave the job over and almost collapsed on the ground, another fireman came up carrying a defibrillator, but Helen was already beginning to breathe on her own. They started first aid for the other injuries.

The Ambulance was the next to arrive, the Fire brigade and Ambulance people were all volunteers and it'd taken time to get from their regular jobs to the vehicles, they took one look at Helen's injuries and called for the rescue Helicopter from Hamilton.

"You'll be taken to the Hospital in Thames" the Ambulance officer told Sandy. "The other, more serious injury will be taken down to Hamilton, that's where the spinal and neurological unit is"

"How bad is she?" Sandy was worried.

"Fractured Vertebrae in the neck, I can't say if the spinal column has been affected yet" the ambulance officer, a young girl with a ponytail and gentle manner replied. Sandy was impressed with this girl as she seemed younger than her, but was taking all this carnage 'in her stride' yet able to care for those still needing the care. "Then there's a couple of fractured ribs, broken pelvis and two broken legs" the girl had finished her examination of Sandy and apart from the dislocated shoulder, a few deep bruises that had originally had them thinking 'internal bleeding' and a sprained ankle that would need binding up for a couple of days she was 'good to go'

The Police had been the last of the three to show up, the operator had mobilized the three services in the order they would be needed with the Fire brigade first, then the Ambulance and lastly the Police to take statements and take over 'traffic management.' The Police was one 'copper', a senior constable (by the looks of the rank insignia on the uniform) who headed straight down to the McLaren, just as he got there another two squad cars arrived and began setting up a traffic cordon, they were going to close the road until the McLaren was recovered, and a scene examination was done, a tow truck was on the way.

Joey'd made his way back to Sandy who was getting first aid by a very attentive fireman, that is until Joey showed up, and then he became a little more 'businesslike'.

He sat down beside Sandy and put his arm around her, she was in shock and looked totally numb.

The St John's Ambulance staff had taken over the treatment for the three of them, Helen had been stabilized and the rescue helicopter was on its way. "It's ten minutes away" the paramedic treating Sandy had said, she was a quiet and efficient worker, Joey wondered what she did in her normal job. 'Probably a helpful sales assistant' he thought to himself.

They'd been given thermal blankets to wrap around themselves, Joey gave his up and wrapped it round Sandy, she didn't seem to notice, all he could hear from her was "I'm sorry, I'm so sorry"

"Hey" Joey spoke softly to her. "It wasn't your fault!" She just looked at him as he gently put his arm around her. Sandy wasn't one to show emotions, she usually kept them bottled up inside, afraid that if they got out people would think less of her, but somehow it was just different with Joey. Around him she felt safe. She felt she could show her true self even with the emotional baggage. Instead of pulling away like she'd do with anyone else she turned and moved closer into him feeling safe.

The dam that that was her emotions and had withstood so much in the past would have ruptured, flooding everything in it's path, but she'd found one with whom she could open the 'sluice gates' of emotion and relieve the pressure; the dam would not break while Joey was there to turn to. She simply turned towards him and the tears quietly began to come.

It was a full five minutes before he heard those tears subside, he didn't interrupt or say anything, truth was he had no idea what to say anyway, he just sat there quietly trying to think of something to say, yet knowing whatever he said just wouldn't be adequate. Finally as the tears subsided he heard Sandy's voice quietly say "Thank you"

He almost asked "What for?" as he'd no idea what he should be doing or saying, yet it seemed the right thing to do, instead he just said, "You're welcome."

They were still holding each other when one of the police approached, he was fairly young looking. 'Probably not long out of Police College' was their initial reaction. Black hair, brown eyes, muscular build standing about five nine in height 'rugby build's Joey guessed. "Which one, union or league?" He asked.

"Huh" the cop was a bit thrown by the question, he was meant to be the one asking questions. "League" he replied. "How'd you work that out?"

"Sorry, just very observant" Joey replied in an almost apologetic tone, the last thing he wanted was to annoy this guy; he was only here to take statements after all.

"Thank you for your patience" the cop began, "I'm officer" he began, it wasn't like they were going anywhere, but at least he was being polite, just trying to help what he must have thought were two shattered and terrified tourists, Sandy still had a bit of a vacant look about her but Joey was quietly watching everything, taking all the details in. "My name's officer Kingi and I'll be starting your statements, just the basics then the senior constable will 'run through them with you later, when you've had time to compose yourselves, did either of you see the car before the crash?"

"Oh" they both replied almost in unison, it was odd as police normally like to get the statements properly at the start and only go over them if there's a discrepancy, at least that's what the movies show. It was almost as if the sergeant was saying "I don't trust you" at the start.

"I saw everything." It was Joey spoke up. "The car came round the corner doing at least a hundred," he began.

"Kilometres?" Officer Kingi asked.

"No, miles" Joey replied, "Take a look at the tyre tracks on the road, you'll see they're way bigger than they'd be for someone doing a mere sixty miles an hour" he pointed to the skid marks they could see from where they were sat. "He was still accelerating, but trying like crazy to stop which was nuts, he was bricking himself" Joey saw the cop look confused, "I mean scared shitless"

'Never heard that one before" the cop replied, glancing up from his notes,"but point taken now"

The next ten minutes was taken up with Joey recounting the encounter in graphic detail, he noticed that the copper was wearing a name badge saying 'Hene', his full name was 'Hene Kingi,' Joey filed that information away in his brain for 'future use' but the copper was having problems accepting all that Joey was telling him, it's well known that people can make things up so they seem more important than they really are in an investigation, he wondered if Joey was doing that.

"You seem pretty sure of what happened" Hene began, "are you sure of what you're telling me?"

"Absolutely" Joey replied without any hint of offence, "I'm used to dealing with high stress situations"

"This is a little more than just as 'high' stress situation" Hene started to reply, 'Fatal crashes usually"

"Are usually the worst" Joey finished the reply. "In my line of work I'm used to dealing with them, and often dealing with fatalities as well"

Just as they were wrapping the statements up one of the Ambulance crew came back towards them, they'd managed to carry Helen down a little way and two of the crew along with the Doctor and Paramedic from the Helicopter rescue unit were busy strapping her into the back of the helicopter, as soon as she was strapped in the doctor and paramedic climbed into the back, the engine pitch changed and the vessel began to rise as soon as the door was closed.

"They're taking the Lady to Waikato Hospital" the crew person, the petite blonde who'd treated them earlier explained. "We'll take you to Thames for treatment, and then arrange for transport for you to get to her"

"Thank you" Sandy was grateful. She didn't really want to be separate from her sister right at this moment, but there was no way they'd all fit into the machine, and Helen really needed the urgent attention. "There's no need though, just point us to where we can hire a car for a little while"

It was just then that Sandy's phone buzzed, they'd forgotten that when she called the Ambulance someone else had listened in to the call, it was them texting now, the message was simple and said "Report in ASAP!"

If you enjoyed the story
Then follow the link below and you'll get
regular updates as well as a weekly post from me
lawrence'sletters@wordress.com

Other books by me

Scorpion Team series

1. **Scorpion's Reach**
2. **Scorpion's Vengeance**

Just a little note.
I hope that you've enjoyed the story here, and
wouldn't mind if I asked you for a little favour.
See, Amazon love to find out what their
readers think of the products people buy.

They do this by asking you to rate it using a star system, one star for "Yeah, Mah" or whatever and Five stars for "WOW, this was AWESOME!"

Can I ask you to take the time to do the 'star thing'? All you have to do is click on the one on the left for the one star, or the one on the right for the five stars, clicking in between will give it ratings wherever you click.

Thanks for that.

Oh and by the way, write a little comment about what worked or didn't work for you.

Thanks again.

Lawrence

Printed in Poland
by Amazon Fulfillment
Poland Sp. z o.o., Wrocław

51045769R00112